SKY ROBERT

A Reverse Harem Alien Romance

Broken Books

Kent, WA 98030

First published in the United States of America by Broken Books LLC, 2025

ISBN: 978-1-963669-02-2

Cover Design by Open World Cover Designs

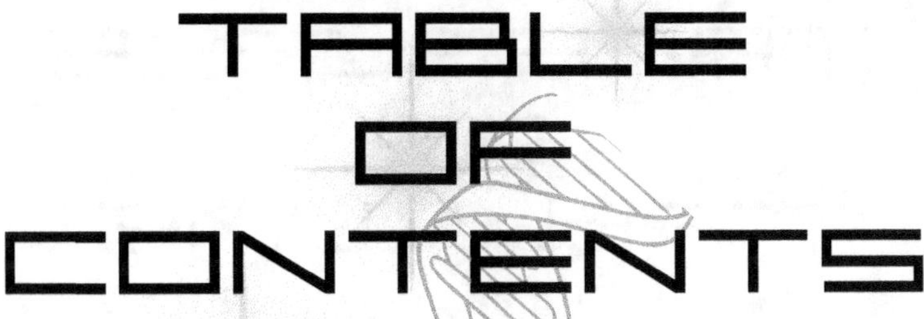

TABLE OF CONTENTS

HTTPS://BOOKS.STEVIEMARIE.COM/HERALIENEXCHANGE
HTTPS://BOOKS.STEVIEMARIE.COM/HERALIENSAVIOR
HTTPS://BOOKS.STEVIEMARIE.COM/HERALIENWARRIOR

HTTPS://BOOKS.STEVIEMARIE.COM/JOTAB
HTTPS://BOOKS.STEVIEMARIE.COM/HERALIENPRINCE
HTTPS://BOOKS.STEVIEMARIE.COM/HERALIENINSURGENT
HTTPS://BOOKS.STEVIEMARIE.COM/HERALIENSTAR

COMING SOON

ALL BOOKS:
STEVIEMARIE.COM

Trillume Universe Glossary

All the books in the Trillume Universe are standalone romances, but if you like to know context before diving in this glossary is for you. This glossary is not necessary to enjoy the books. It's simply a tool for those who like to refer to it for further explanations or reminders of alien terminology.

Her Alien Delegate is a REVERSE HAREM – fated mates alien romance. There are MMMF spicy scenes, including double pen, tentacles, and breeding kink. The FMC does become pregnant in the end, but unGor pregnancies take years to gestate, so there is no birth or offspring in this book. There are mating marks, kink harness play, fangs, and fullness/stretching.

Don't forget to grab Her Alien Exchange, a full-length spicy space vampire romance, for free here, this story is a parallel timeline to this story: https://books.steviemarie.com/heralienexchange

Necia warriors: from the planet Necias Prime. Centuries ago, the trill from Trillume came to their planet and took control through the tribal laws to conquer their planet through manipulation. There is an unstated understanding that if the necia did not submit to the new rule that many lives would have been lost in a hostile takeover. This species is very open about their sexuality and anything pertaining to what is considered normal biological needs; this includes their species accepting exhibitionist/voyeuristic culture as it is life threatening to not keep their bodies in balance with sharing fluids like blood and sexual release. There is blood play, primal play, and many honor traditions within the tribe. They have an exoskeleton under what they call their second skin (the first layer of skin) that protrudes like spikes that they call EPUL from their skin, making them a lethal weapon, their second skin hardens when threatened. Human-like in appearance, though they are larger in stature with their extra bone structure, they have retractable fangs, and their peens have epul nodes (not sharp) that extend and fill, while also being the means that they knot and impart their D.N.A. into their chosen mate. They also have an epul that extends from the base of their shaft like a tuning fork which pushes out as their skin pulls taut and perfectly reaches a human female's clit. Though they are open sexually, once they bond with a mate, they are loyal and dedicated lovers.

UnGor warriors: From the planet AsunGor. unGor is lowercased similar to human. The planet has harsh winds that make life above the surface difficult. Much of the species live beneath the surface, with beautifully carved tunnel systems, and even domes allowing for a view of the surface, though the skies are difficult to see beyond what they know as the Dan Star, or the Red Star to mark rotations of time.

Gengaktor: A mating ceremony of proving worthy of bonding on AsunGor, often displaying skills, or providing a venue for a mate to hear the stories of accomplishment that an unGor warrior cannot speak about themselves without diminishing their deeds.

Ormete: the AsunGor strands of hair, that fuse together in dreadlocks but feel very much like smooth tentacles. These tentacles contain many nerves and can be controlled as one would their own fingers. They are often ornamented with bones or trophies of accomplishments in the clan and can vibrate or glow when bonded with a mate. Some strands will remain thin like threads, but the nerves in those ormete are not as strong and are more difficult to control beyond looking like windless ghost hair capable of billowing with no air to lift it. The nerves in the ormete have a luminescence about them, meaning they are the reason why their hair can glow when reacting to a mate bond. In terms of looks, the tentacles look like human hair, except they feel like skin, and when fused they are thicker, forming more cartilage and capable of squeezing strong enough to break bones.

Waustenger: a dangerous water creature that can be mistaken for a rock, often surprising unwary warriors in the cenotes of AsunGor.

Nephec: A sharp-toothed creature in AsunGor's caverns.

Necia/Necias: necia is lowercased similar to human. Necias is capitalized as it references a short phrase for the planet a proper name.

Necia Delta Fal: an outlaw planet ruled by King Sylve when he abandoned his home planet.

Epul: the spikes that protrude from the second skin of a necia warrior

Epulknot: what necia call their peen

Epulslip: What necia call female pussy

Ellopul: What necia call come

Galactic Trill Authority: a council of diplomats that oversee the rule of the universe, like many overseeing bodies there is corruption as well as decent aliens

Ganpan-fal: world destroyer

Human Exchange Trade: H.E.T.

Pulsunne: a fated mate in necia culture, means heart's song in their tongue

Rakture: Ancient battle for mating rights of the necia tribe

Rutting: sex/fucking in necia culture

Rut: a condition with necia warriors where their adrenaline must be balanced by the act of copulation to regulate their body's chemistry.

Chapter One

Mate for Sale

"She's a viperous demon that prefers the company of books over preparing a meal, but what she lacks in culinary skills, she makes up for in apt listening. She is not bad on the eyes and I have found humans require little to maintain," my alien husband announced to the bazaar that he had said we were going to because he had something "special" planned for me.

When I joined the alien exchange for a mate match, I didn't have too much in the way of expectations. It was guaranteed I would be treated well no matter which alien selected me, and divorces weren't a thing on Trillume. If we didn't match well, I was told that another mate could be selected, or I could be returned to Earth. There were plenty of other exchange opportunities for humans. We were one of the few species in the galaxy who defended ourselves with tools instead of any biological advantages like claws, sharp fangs, poison, or thick hides. We had none of them, and this apparently made us commodities with other aliens because we were not a threat. Some thought us similar to pets, and others liked feeling superior with their scales, and the fact that they could subdue most species with a touch of their skin.

"What?" I huffed under my breath in disbelief at what I was hearing. I was pretty sure I heard him say I was a demon for not joining him to make food. He made it seem like he enjoyed cooking. Plus, he would have been aware from my file that I had no skills in that area, let alone with new food sources from this planet. Was he irritated that I didn't come to the kitchen to cook with him? Maybe he wanted to share his love of food and was going to teach me things, but that was not how it came across.

Now, what? He was calling me a demon because I decided to stay in the library to wait for him?

I was looking up any texts on Trillume culture and trying to learn more about it, but now we were here at some kind of auction house while he paraded me around leering aliens. He kept his hood over his head to hide his features, yet his claws waved about towards the crowd and back towards me.

We had hardly been married for more than a week, or really seven sleeps because Earth time wasn't quite the same. Everything was finalized during my trip to Trillume, and I wasn't exactly sure what was happening until my translator was picking up on bidding amounts after my husband's list of pros and cons of having me around, after only knowing me for a short time.

The price increased passed the amount of the allowance I was being granted for an entire year of joining the mating program. I didn't have much time left to be considered a prime candidate, as my file was labeled geriatric, and I had a history of miscarriages. Guess that's what I was, being in my thirties now, and with no children to prove I wasn't sterile. I wasn't about to pop out a kid just to prove to some file that I wasn't broken, but I wouldn't lie that starting a family was the deciding factor to join, it didn't hurt that they would pay for all the debts I'd gained trying to start my own family with human treatments alone.

Now that I was part of the exchange program, I had access to alien technology that would prolong my life and allow me to have a family. Honestly, I was probably younger than a teenager on Earth in terms of viable lifespan from all the alien inoculations I've had in order to travel in space.

Before I could have a conversation with my husband, Ter-ak, a female with bright pink hair and gems along her arms placed the highest bid. She waved her hand and I could hear Ter-ak behind me confirming her credits cleared verification scans. I spun around to glare at him, but he had already disappeared into the crowd and the tall pink woman was so fast that I didn't even see her stab me with some kind of injection.

I squeaked, unable to say a word. That's how I've always been, the wallflower in the back of the room observing. Even with Ter-ak, I was trying to show him I'd learn to adapt and get to know him by reading up on his culture, since I was too shy to ask him directly. I figured I'd have some time to get comfortable and then show him with my actions, but never got the chance.

I should have studied more about the trill before I agreed to a match, but I was so excited to be selected to leave before I lost my apartment.

With the birthrates on a decline, the only way I would have kept my subsidized room would be to join the breeding program where many of the women in my apartments were required to be inseminated once a quarter to keep their spots after they turned thirty.

That wasn't the way I wanted to spend the rest of my life, but I wasn't even given that choice anymore. I'd spent my extra credits to have control over picking who I had fertility treatments with, but I'd gone into debt not because of choosing my donors, but because I no longer was subsidized to join the breeding program after too many miscarriages. At least with the aliens, I'd know who my baby's daddy was, and I'd be taken care of by the Galactic Authority for life.

At least, that's what I thought until a new alien was taking me away from the bazaar and Ter-ak was nowhere to be seen. Now, everything was uncertain.

The tall pink alien woman must have seen my trembling and she spoke softly so as to not spook me, "I work for the royal science department of the Galactic Authority. It is one of my tasks to regularly attend the Bazaar in the Blue District for this very reason. The trill do not have a... what does your species call a separation of mates?"

"Divorce?"

"Divorce of mates is not done. Those of poor skill and honor will sell their mate's contract to trade the mate to another, as long as you haven't bonded with them. Others may duel for mating as the ancients of this planet did. Your contract has been traded to further research with a compatible species the necia, as that is the wish of who I serve. The prick you felt earlier was to have your blood sample analysis sent to the lab to find a viable mate match for your contract. Contracts are dangerous once the first one is traded."

I didn't say anything. I was still stuck on what exactly that meant for me. Everyone in the H.E.T. program knew that the necia were warriors that helped protect the Trillume Galaxy, but I didn't pry beyond that. Would this match discard me like Ter-ak did? Would they be kind? Would they be upset that I wasn't as talkative or outgoing as some of the other girls I'd met when I first departed for Trillume?

"Everything will be provided for you, and I will send someone to retrieve whatever belongings might have been left with your previous mate, but there isn't much time before the next ship leaving for Necias Prime departs. You are not required to stay with a necia warrior mate. Their mating customs are to protect their mates, and their tribe will hold them to honor that. If you are unhappy with your match, you may return to Earth, but you must give the warrior a chance to prove his honor before making this decision."

What exactly did that mean? How was I supposed to give the warrior a chance? I didn't believe I was given a chance here on Trillume with Ter-ak.

"Is there an option to stay on Trillume?" I finally found my voice as she led me away through the alleys and shops popped up along the streets. She adjusted her hood to cover her pink hair, and I copied her just in case it was prudent to do so when we were by ourselves in what she called the Blue District. Blue was a color associated with no access on most alien ships here, and likely indicated that it wasn't just a bazaar, but a place of unscrupulous types that didn't care whether I had a contract or not.

"Ah, yes," she said suddenly. "You are a match for a warrior who has already signed a contract with us that he has yet to fulfill. He has agreed to honor any suitable mate prospect for one Earth year, after which your contract will return you to Earth unless you decide to bond and complete your... marriage. That is the Earth's word for this, yes?"

So, she was saying that he wouldn't actually be my husband until after a year of being his mate, if I wanted him to be?

"And if I return to Earth?" I squeaked.

"You will be compensated for your service to the exchange, and you may apply for other contract opportunities. The contract transfer you have with the trade commission is clear that unless you are mated, you must be returned to Earth. As your mating with the trill was transferred to an uncompleted mate prospect, you have one Earth year to complete the bond per your mate's customs.

"Once you are bonded, completing the contract, it cannot be traded so easily. That is the one universal law of mating contracts. Until you have completed the marriage contract terms, your contract is at risk of being stolen or sold by any unscrupulous outlaw around."

I chewed on my lip nervously and nodded my understanding. This was a blessing that she had bought my contract instead of someone else. If I was understanding correctly, the necia warrior would have already been my husband if he bought the contract directly, regardless of what I wanted. By having the Galactic Authority be the go-between, I have a year to decide for myself and will be returned to Earth if I'm not happy with it.

As if she could see where my head was going, she added, “It’s important that you know that this is more than a typical exchange contract. We are conducting research on the compatibility of humans and necia warriors that could solve the fertility crisis across many different species. Consider giving this warrior a chance to prove his honor. The necia warriors are good to their mates. Others may be too modest to say so.

"The trill are so tight-lipped about many things, but even if you do not wish him as a mate, we can gather needed data from your physical responses to the warrior’s rut. This can be used as a valuable asset that you can barter a new contract with researchers such as myself and who I work for. A research contract is safer than keeping your current mating contract incomplete.”

“Rut?”

“You have enough compatibility that it is likely you will trigger a rut with the warrior. You are functioning properly to mate, are you not?”

“I—I,” I choked on my own spit as I gulped with embarrassment. Of course, I was physically able to do the sheet tango, but it was always understood that I was in charge of when I felt comfortable to do that. She was saying that I would trigger a frenzy, and that frightened me so much that I froze.

She bent over and held my cheeks in her warm hands to get my attention back to her. “Evie, that is your name, is it not? You will have a few Earth weeks to contact your future mate before you meet in the flesh. Get to know him, begin your bond here,” she placed her palm to my head, "and here." Her jeweled fingers cupped together over my heart and glowed. She wasn't a trill, and I didn't know what kind of species she was, but she was beautiful and being around her kept the chill from the air away.

"The next ship to Necias Prime will leave in seven sleeps. We will stay in a private room here in the Blue District until departure where you can be taught about the necia customs from the AI here."

I nodded, as we entered a dome-like building, though when we passed the sliding doors we were scanned by a laser.

"It's verifying our identities," she assured before we passed through another door that had a wall of masks and a screen of options in the trill language that I definitely couldn't read, but the pictures were enough to make me anxious. There was a slide show of what I assumed were different alien genitalia on display. When I squeaked, my escort hurriedly looked around as if there were a threat in the room that startled me until she glanced between the screen and me then sighed. "Many of these rooms are filled with those seeking to pleasure themselves. They come for the thrill of being chosen or the thrill of the hunt, but our room is not accessible to anyone else. It is simply the least likely place anyone will look for a human before your transport."

"We're hiding?"

"Just until the next shipment of human exchanges arrive from Earth. Word will spread of a human seen at the bazaar.

And in this district, we can't be too careful that others won't try to take you."

"Right..." I said with a shiver. Heat seemed to radiate off of her, so I knew it wasn't the chill of the air. My future was in the hands of this unknown alien woman that worked for the Galactic Authority, as far as I knew.

We passed by door after door along a glowing hallway with red lights above each one until we came to the end where a few blue lit doors remained and an open door that led to what appeared to be an elevator. My escort stopped at one of the blue doors and pressed her hand into the scanner outside. Air wheezed as the door decompressed and slid open.

She pointed to the door to reassure me. "Blue is occupied and not accepting visitors. No one can enter but the one that rests here. Please place your hand on the scanner."

I lifted it like she did and the blue light blinked before flashing red, then blue again.

"It is now your room," she explained. "I must leave you to attend to my duties, but will return to check on you. Remain in your room for your safety. All necessary needs are provided inside, as well as a tablet that you may use to reach me, as well as your future mate. You may uplink those contacts to your implant for future needs. This is the safest place to be until your transport. No one may enter without your approval, but please be careful. This place may not divulge who or what you are, but it knows and will still sell your scent and even the sounds you make for other's enjoyment. Do not give your approval for anything."

I gulped as the door slid closed behind me and the sound of locking mechanisms clicked in place. What was this place?

"Welcome to the Blue District," my implant spoke. I assumed the facility connected with my implant when it scanned me. "We hold the largest selection of species for your pleasure, company, and research. Please utilize the screen to your right as you wish. Masks are most common for sampling different scents with more precision. One is provided in every room to filter scents by room.

"Any room with a golden glow is open; simply apply your biomarker to enter and it will change the room's glow to blue to signal occupied. There are a few species that prefer to scan your metrics for compatibility before entering; these rooms are identified with a green glow."

Blue was the color of an occupied room, and the corridors I'd seen on entry were mostly golden, a few green, and towards the end many were blue. The halls were in several shades of blue, both from the glow of lights, and the color of the doors, a blueish-purple metal.

The voice returned to my implant as I approached the screen to the right and said, "Please enjoy your stay here and follow the laws of the Blue District. Damaging any species while on the premises is strictly forbidden. We understand there are varying degrees of what is considered damaging among species, so please refer to the species chart for clarification, accessed through all implants during your stay. Your implant has been approved for this single room for seven sleep cycles, including reentries, no time limits. Several floors are currently under construction. Please remain on floors six through thirty-four should you decide to browse our selected services. This floor is reserved for long-term tenants and must not be disturbed without pre-authorization from your terminal."

There was a lot to unpack from this greeting. I stared at tablet on the wall in shock for longer than I cared to admit.

Welcome to the Blue District, indeed.

Chapter Two
Broma

Blood dripped down my jaw where my very own adornment weaved through my ormete braid was used to tear into my scalp, hoping to cut off its source. That was my fault for thinking I could throw the duel without consequences. This wasn't some mere sibling rivalry.

He was my brother, in more than name, but blood from our mother ran through his veins as well. He would not accept the commission to lead our tribes without my full effort in this duel to prove he was worthy of protecting our interests across the entire planet of AsunGor. Mother had no daughters to give the commission to. The top candidates would fight for the honor. As her blood, I had no right to refuse and am forced to fight my way towards the honored role of leadership. But I did not want such responsibility.

It was unfortunate to have my first duel be against Brakaun. Even more unfortunate that he did not wish to win by my disinterest alone. He would threaten my ormete and a future with any delegate by cutting it from my scalp. The only thing that kept me from killing him immediately was that he had tried to do it with a sharpened bone from my first groka hunt as a youngling, attached to the end of my ormete. This meant he was warning me what he would do if I didn't take the duel seriously, but he knew he would not be able to follow through with the threat with such a dull instrument. The last time I sharpened that bone was the day I added it to my braid. It was dull from too many cycles passed.

"You would threaten to dishonor me?" I seethed, after barely escaping the cut that would have shaved my ormete at the root. A wound so deep would mean I'd never grow them back, and I would never duel again.

"I do nothing that you weren't willing to do to me. Is it not dishonorable to throw a duel with such importance as Commissioner of AsunGor?"

My ormete wrapped around his hand, preventing him from continuing to put pressure on the bone pressed to my forehead. The strain from disuse was a disadvantage, but a duel among unGor was never just about the strength of our ormete, but in how we handled struggle. Many of my brothers have forgotten this, but not Brakaun. He was honorable and wanted a just win.

Slipping under the assault, I released my ormete when I was out of the way, allowing the bone to cut across my forehead before Brakaun's fist plunged forward through the air. His palm dripped from the force he held the bone as it slid through his grip. This was a sign that he too was merciful and just in his decisions, because he could have held firm and torn through my ormete's flesh by keeping the bone in his fist. The bone would have torn through, cutting my ormete in half from where it was pierced through towards the ends. The damage wouldn't have ripped my ormete from the root, but it would have made that part of my braid unusable for many cycles as it healed. It would mean I would not be able to duel again for this commission.

Two times he has shown our mother and the elders of his firm yet merciful leadership, while I have shown them first that I did not wish to rule and was willing to be humiliated to concede my power to a worthy warrior. What kind of leader would that make me? I wondered as his own ormete swung out to wrap around my neck. His first adornment was from a curved tooth of a nephek shark, as he was favored by our finest sea merchant, learning the art of battle while within our underground cenote.

He would win a duel between us if it came down to who could keep their breath longer, so yet again I was forced to dodge his attack, but I was already mid-motion of avoiding the last one. I had to lift my arm to hook the tooth around my wrist, cutting into my flesh, before I could twist it and grip his ormete above and yanked. It was that or expose my neck to him.

"Too hasty," I chided him as I dug my claws into his ormete. "You underestimated my own mercy. For I have none."

I'd lose this duel for leadership, but I would be showing the clans that I would not be merciful should someone duel me in the future. It would deter other warriors from trying to make a name for themselves at the cost of my honor.

His roar echoed across the crowd as I ripped a chunk of his ormete strands off at his shoulders using the sharp tooth within his own braid. It would take him some time to heal and grow that length back, but as long as there wasn't someone who challenged his leadership, he'd still become the next Commissioner of AsunGor.

"You waustenger!" The creature in the water that hid in the cracks to deceitfully lure prey close and then to eat them alive. They had the same appearance as the rock and were considered betrayers of the deep, with no allegiances to anyone but themselves.

I had made one my second trophy, carving an adornment from their stoney flesh after killing one with my bare claws. The sound it made still sent chills down my legs.

"Brothers should not duel unless it is to bring them closer and solve disputes, not cause them." I took my own ormete braid and settled it within the curve of the tooth I had removed from his own ormete, then allowed the sharpened weapon to slice it off.

The pain was so severe, I nearly dropped to my knees, seeing only the whites of my eyes. It was only by will alone that I stood, though unsteadily, to drop my ormete and his own on his lap before I heard my mother's word to end the duel echo in my ears, "Enough!"

"He's touched by a demon," a whisper reached my consciousness through the haze as I walked away.

"Fearless," another said with awe.

"Take a knee, you fool. He will be the next Commissioner of AsunGor," a deep male's voice, that I recognized as Pheyal snapped to someone next to him, but all I could see was the next step in front of the other as I left the Commissioner's Arena. It would be broadcast to all the clans across the planet of what I had done.

"Aren't you going to duel him next?"

"I have no need to. I will follow Broma even if they choose his brother to lead, as will every clan that has seen an unGor willing to destroy himself to seek a future where no warrior would dare to reproach him unless what they fight for is worth losing their ormete. It will bring peace between clans, and a story worth spreading throughout the galaxy that would strengthen our trade and protect our planet."

A story worth spreading across the galaxy, I thought about what Pheyal spoke of, and then I felt my weight buckle my legs beneath me. Large arms held me up and Pheyal spoke again, "It makes a better story if you keep your feet grounded until you get to your room. I'll bring the poultice that clots the bleeding of your ormete." My body was hoisted in the air as he roared through the crowd for me like I'd already been crowned the next commissioner.

His roar was echoed through the crowd until all I heard were the calls of the unGor across the arena.

When I woke next, I was presented with the bones I had collected since my youth. Each one was a memory of growth, and in them was a new one that was never mine, the tooth of the nephek.

"This one is not mine," I told Pheyal.

"Brakaun has awoken. He said it was not his anymore. It should serve you as you lead AsunGor."

"Lead AsunGor?"

"It has been decided. Every clan commissioner has kneeled down. Your duel with your blood brother was to determine who the clan leaders would challenge for commission of the planet. No clan wishes to challenge you."

"It is because of you Pheyal," another male spoke up from behind him.

I turned my attention to see a warrior in medical robes and even his ormete were adorned with bones that were gifted to him from warriors whose lives he saved, not from the hunt. They were each carved with different signatures.

"This is my brood mate, Vaquel. He has been with me since his blood brother never returned from recovering their mother Delegate Quezet. The whole commission went in search of her, never to return. He was left in my mother's care and has been by my side since." It was obvious that Pheyal was changing the subject.

"Pheyal kneeled and showed the clans he would follow you, then every clan commissioner present and through vids accepted his choice as their own," Vaquel said, ignoring the way Pheyal growled in displeasure. It was true that having Pheyal's acceptance was an honor, as he was the most likely to win a duel for succession. I'd never met him before, but his reputation was known throughout AsunGor.

"I see," I acknowledged. "I'll have a word with Trema in reinstating your duel for commissioner of the estate."

"I do not seek it," he grumbled back.

My hand lifted to hold the ache in my skull at bay. No medpack was used to speed my recovery and this could only mean Pheyal believed I would wish to keep the scar as a mark of my victory.

"I've added a poultice to ease the pain, but if you want to have use of your ormete again, it's best to not disturb the stitching

I've done with any medbots. Better to suffer the process than have them be nothing more than decoration," it was Vaquel that spoke and held up a glass jar that he pulled from his robe sleeve.

"He has studied much from a scientist on Trillume. Given how freshly cut the injury, Vaquel believes that you and your brother will have full use of your ormete again," Pheyal said with pride.

"You mustn't strain them until they are fully healed," Vaquel warned. "No lifting, pulling, or anything that could damage the repaired area. You could permanently damage them."

I stared at the ornaments in front of me, yet there was a weight to my head that was more than the cut across my forehead and down my brow ridge.

"This has never been done before," I regarded in wonder, but still in disbelief. My ormete were still wrapped, being held up with bandages, leaving me to imagine that they weren't sheared short because of my own actions. I thought I would have to wait many cycles to not appear like a youth with short ormete strands. "How?" Ormete strands were so fine until they were braided together, that repairing them had never been attempted.

"It's just lucky that you didn't cut too close to the scalp. The ormete absorb together, fusing—and the lower on the braid the more likely it is to be repaired as the ormete are larger and the blood vessels have become one where they've attached."

"One inch shorter and you would have had to live with that decision for many cycles," Pheyal added.

"He still may," Vaquel corrected.

There was still much healing to do before there was any certainty about my ormete's future.

"Trema is waiting to give you the first mark of suns, then you will visit every leader for their formal blessing."

Reaching for my robes, I stopped to touch the bandages on my head. It wasn't how I imagined my future to be, being responsible for the planet and its diplomacy across the galaxy.

When I entered the tent of my mother, Trema of AsunGor, she had quickly waved her hand to clear an image projected onto the pulled Isot skin. Though we had technology, including implants, we stayed close to our roots and used it sparingly for off-world negotiations, trade, and communication between the clan estates.

"I was under the impression that you were marking me today, and secrets of estate would be revealed," I said nonchalantly as I sat on the cushioned pillow on the ground of layered carpets.

"You are right," she said with a laugh. "Old habits are hard to change. I never wanted to worry you or your brothers, but we never were blessed with a sister. None of the clans wished to part with their own female leadership, and after your stunt in dueling your brother... you've created a story they are proud to share, but it comes with a price."

I waited for her to discuss the price my display cost the planet.

"No delegates are interested in mating with you. You will be nothing more than a figurehead that protects our planet in name alone. Your brother has been offered to join the delegation of the Faust clan, and should he father a female, she will succeed you upon her first coming-of-age ceremony."

I nodded my understanding. This wasn't something I was against, and I prayed my brother would have many blessings in his new delegation.

"You have caught the attentions of Pheyal, and he wishes to grant you a delegation within his clan, but that isn't possible without a mate of your own. I've arranged for you to seek delegation through a human contract that you will pick up from Trillume personally."

"So soon?" I sat up straighter, confused about how quickly she was able to secure a mating contract when I had only just dueled.

"It was planned for whoever lost the duel long before you fought, but negotiations for a contract with no end date took time to secure. I hadn't thought it would be needed for my son that gained the support of the clans and that the one not leading would secure a mate first." She sighed with exhaustion.

My head bowed with what I knew was disappointment. I had dishonored her by trying to forfeit the duel, and winning the commission through notoriety was not what she had wanted for me.

"No human has accepted the mating contract yet," she clarified, "but Trillume has guaranteed me that the humans have accepted the terms and are simply seeking a match. Head to Trillume to be ready to retrieve her when she arrives. There have been too many mishaps with losing humans who are not escorted properly, and our clan estates are dwindling without an influx of delegates. You will lead the way for more of our warriors to apply for a commission of estate and be chosen by a delegate."

"It is unusual to have a delegate agree to mate without having met them," I said with disbelief.

I never had any choice of being a commissioner. If I had, then I would not have been here feeling the throb of my ormete healing. Being within my mother's clan meant that I was always around when she dealt with territory issues or disputes. While she was more secretive about diplomacy among the stars, she taught many lessons on getting to know our trade partners and knowing customs outside of our own.

My mother's robes brushed across the ground as she approached with a bottle of her blood mixed with crushed Grotbug to turn it black. She kneeled down beside me and patted above my chest.

"Of my heart, I give you blood of your ancestors that may guide you in leading AsunGor into new prosperity. Not only in wealth, but in health as we grow." She dipped a nail into the black ink and proceeded to mark me with AsunGor's great star cluster that holds us within its many suns each clan is named for. Only through the domes could any of us see the suns above our planet. The winds were too great to see them clearly on the surface.

"Dig deep and where we once were is greater still than the stars," I prayed as I placed my fist to her heart as I was unable to offer her my ormete.

Her claws dug into my skin, the ink burning its mark on me. The ground up shell of the hugput bug reacted to our blood, causing a hardened decay where my mother's claw carved the stars in my skin. My mark would be stronger, but it would never heal. No medpack or technology could undo it without first removing the damage.

It was a common ingredient to use if we wished to keep our scars or to stop bleeding immediately.

"You must quickly bond with a delegate before your brother succeeds with the Yukatra tribe. He was accepted by Commissioner Akili, but bonding takes time, especially since he is not officially delegated to her, and she has others that must also accept him."

"I don't understand."

What was she trying to tell me?

She stopped marking my chest to brush aside my bandage from my forehead. Clucking her tongue she then closed her eyes as if the look of what she saw under the wrapping hurt to see. "Your position as Commissioner of AsunGor is not without its dangers, and being unbonded makes those dangers greater. You're lucky that the hugput paste was already rubbed off before you cut your own ormete. Your brother's ormete could not be recovered. His blood burned up the hugput before you cut your own."

"Hugput?"

"The tooth was freshly sharpened and covered in hugput paste before your duel," she said with measured words like we were speaking about what to eat for dinner.

"He intended to harm me permanently," I processed out loud.

She carefully dipped her nail into the ink and returned to marking my skin. I hissed as it burned, now very much not in control of my reactions.

My mother lifted a brow at my pain, and I sucked in a breath to measure my own emotions. There was no place for such things when I held the responsibility of all unGor on my shoulders. She nodded, then continued.

"You may be thinking why I allow him an honor of joining any commission after fooling our tribes into believing he was fighting fairly," I opened my mouth to speak, but she shook her head to let her explain more, "I will not tell anyone that the duel was compromised, because you were able to handle it, and it gives you the opportunity to rule in your own way on how to handle your brother, and his inevitable future actions to take control."

"If you know then, why?"

"Should I answer that for you?" She challenged.

"If you handled it, then I would lose trust within the tribes and my brother would gain more support. Our planet is at peace and ripe for misplaced dissatisfaction that could cause tribal wars."

"It pleases me that you have listened to me over the years. You will find a way to quell your brother's greed and secure your place as leader of our tribes."

"With a delegate," I surmised.

"It is the safest way. Not that it is the only way."

"Kill him..."

"It isn't that simple," she said with an exhausted sigh. "If that is what you choose to do, I will support you, even if it pains my heart."

"But..." I knew there was more.

"But—killing him does not fix things. Some will praise you for your dedication to rule without favoritism. Others..."

"Others would see me as weak, and unworthy of leadership if I couldn't even earn the respect of a brother."

"Many would know power corrupts, but they would question if it was your brother or you who has been corrupted."

"I would never—"

She stopped me from defending myself with a direct stare that I'd often seen when either of us were up to mischief when we were younger. "No need. I know all too well that you do not want any of this. I am the one that forced you to duel. There is no law that says you must succeed me to the commission. I ordered you to duel because I could not trust your brother to do it without you."

In a show of emotion I rarely saw from my mother, she cleared her throat to continue, "I didn't know he would resort to hugput on his ormete bones. It permanently damages them when in contact with blood. Such a foolishly risky thing to do when he could have easily harmed himself just as easily as harming you. I have wronged you..."

My teeth ground together, knowing what she didn't say at the end. She wasn't sorry to have wronged me, simply sorry I had been hurt in the process. Her next words confirmed it.

"You've done well with your brother. Your mercy will be remembered, and you've shown the tribes that you're willing to do whatever it takes to protect them. Cutting your own ormete took away any claim your brother would have had to seek vengeance. No warrior would support his actions without a delegate to lead them."

"If the tribes were in such a state of disrest, why are you stepping down?"

"I've grown weary over the cycles, and my last wish is that your brother will understand that being the Commissioner of AsunGor is about bringing the tribes together, not ruling over them. I want you to show every tribe that it isn't one unGor that rules, but all unGor that make us prosper."

All I wanted to do was tend to the Rolly Caverns, and take my brother's offspring on hunting trips for their ormete rites. All of my tribe were brothers, and unmated unGor always helped raise the young. This was all I ever wanted.

"I never intended to have my own delegate..."

"Sometimes our paths are not sought, but given. You must head to Trillume to register with them about your new status as Commissioner of AsunGor. All commissioners visit the Trill Council and help secure diplomacy for our planet before they return. You can meet up with Romek, who can show you around and help you study your new duty to AsunGor, and keep an eye on when a human delegate will be selected for you."

"I'll leave immediately."

"Romek lives on Trillume. He's a strong warrior, but he hasn't seen much outside Trillume for too long," Pheyal advised as the ship was filled with trade goods destined for Trillume. "He has adopted many trill mannerisms, including the vision that he is what you are to AsunGor, a commissioner of all tribes. He may view you as a rival to his claims, and without his support, you are sure to lose respect with the rest of the tribes, which is why I will be joining you."

"What about your tribe?"

Being the commissioner of all AsunGor meant I had no tribe of my own, and Pheyal was still the leader of his own tribe.

Vaquel scoffed like I should know the answer already. I had a feeling he was not as pleased with me as Pheyal was, but it was obvious his loyalties were strong for his tribe.

"Disputes will be addressed to the nearest tribe commissioner, and all commissioners have access to reach us for further consult," Pheyal stated a basic law of a commissioner on leave, but that didn't explain why he was willing to leave for such an extended amount of time, it put his own commission at risk.

"It's important for future bonded brothers to be comfortable with one another. Pheyal should be the second mate in the delegation, and I will be the third," Vaquel spoke directly about my mating contract.

"I cannot guarantee who my mate favors," I reasoned that their expectations were hasty at best. That was one thing I would not learn from my mother. Where she chose her mates diplomatically, and was seldom smiling at any of them, I would not have my mate unhappy.

Being bonded to a delegate wasn't something I had thought much about, but now that I knew I would have one or create an unnecessary diplomatic disaster, or even the death of my brother, I would make sure that she would be happy with our arrangement. Even if she doesn't favor me in our delegation and chooses another first mate, I will support her decision. There was no telling if she would wish to bond with any of us, let alone all three of us. Though a bond with Pheyal and Vaquel would show strength within the commissions across AsunGor.

"I will not dissuade my mate from any bond she chooses, but I will not choose them for her either. This is one thing as first mate I will not interfere with," I explained, watching them both to see if this would change their mind about joining me to Trillume.

"Harmony within a delegation is important," Vaquel objected, but he stopped when Pheyal shook his head.

"This is nothing more than a typical test of worth when joining a delegation; merely the perimeters are different. I will prove myself by gaining her approval," Pheyal said with a determined intensity.

That wasn't exactly supposed to be encouragement to seek out my mate's approval, but there was nothing I could say that would deter Pheyal from seeking to be part of the same commission delegation it seemed. Though, from the look on Vaquel's face, this was not the case for him.

"This is sharply irregular," Vaquel grumbled. "It is easy for one such as Pheyal to accept such conditions to join your delegation, but how am I to impress the delegate into bonding with a tactician? It has been a tradition for every delegation for the first mate to choose one tactician. We aren't chosen by delegates, but endeared towards them through a first mate's approval."

Pheyal replied for me, "And he has made it clear that is how to receive his approval. You will be around often enough to be of use to her before she could possibly bond with other mates." With a mischievous grin, he leaned over towards me to whisper not so subtly, "Vaquel was rather hoping to win our mate over with his other assets in the heat of a bonding ceremony; it is a tradition that many tacticians practice on the har fruit. He's made sure that an extra crate was added to the trade shipment to Trillume."

I nearly coughed on my own saliva at the image of Vaquel applying the right amount of pressure with his tongue to extract the fruit's juices without having it spray out the foul odor. It was normal for some to practice removing the sacks without bursting them, as the oils can spoil the flesh.

"I enjoy the taste of the har fruit," Vaquel defended with a huff. Even I couldn't hold back smiling at Pheyal in agreement that har fruit had a chewy texture and often only used the juice. Seeing we weren't convinced, he continued, "The flesh can be ground up to season the food dispensary meals."

"Yes, adding the unrendered har fruit was to sweeten our meals. A truly thoughtful traveling addition," Pheyal teased.

This was an opportunity to show my interest in bonding with them sincerely. It was clear to me that Pheyal had mentioned this embarrassing topic to promote our future brotherhood.

"It isn't only a skill for tacticians to master. I had no intention of joining a commission, and it wasn't uncommon to see har fruit competitions with winners chosen by females before they become delegates. I'm sure many warriors are chosen to join delegations from those competitions." I tried to sound reassuring, but the assessing stares from both of them told me that I knew too much about these competitions. I refused to backstep my comment, as my mother had taught me confidence and honor were owning both your victories and your failures. Even failures can seem positive when a warrior doesn't shy from them.

"Challenge accepted," Pheyal said while lifting his ormete as an honored agreement for a challenge I had unwittingly given.

Vaquel shifted his weight from boot to boot until Pheyal nudged him forward by tripping him on his extended foot. He smoothly guided the fall with his hand for Vaquel to bow beside him.

"I accept," he choked out with the pressure.

It would be a great disrespect not to take their offered ormete, so I did.

"It is settled," Pheyal said while he stood tall with broad shoulders and a chuckle as he patted Vaquel jovially. "Go fetch the crate from your quarters and let us meet at the dispensaries."

The crate?

Vaquel laughed back at Pheyal; their friendship and bond were obviously strong. "Are we going for speed or precision?"

"There's enough in your crate for both!"

"Don't be upset when you lose," Pheyal taunted then he was gone down the hall to his quarters on the ship.

I watched them with envy as they held an easiness together that I had always craved with my own flesh and blood brother. It wasn't easy to have such freedom when our mother expected one of us to lead in her shadow. The kind of competition between us was never this relaxed.

"Win and I'll consider hosting a delegation recruitment for my mate after we're bonded, though I still won't require her to choose anyone," I offered with a smile. There was no harm in allowing select unGor to show their talents to my mate with a delegation ceremony. She would still have full control over accepting them into the delegation.

Vaquel heard me down the hall and his call echoed back, "Winner gets first claim!"

"You'll lose!" Pheyal called back.

First claim was always an endorsement from the first mate of a delegation.

"And if I win?" I found myself asking with a smirk.

"We'll have to find another way to earn first claim from you. It is the way," Pheyal said while giving me a nudge with his elbow. All these unprovoked touches were attempts to build a bond between us, and already I was feeling myself warming to the idea of having someone to rely on.

Chapter Three
Evie

Waiting inside the Blue District was becoming impossibly frustrating. I've been studying the necia warrior culture from the interface with the AI, but the more I read the more nervous I got. It had been a week, and I'd already forgotten the name of the woman that purchased my contract. She hadn't returned, and I was becoming stir crazy. The credits on my account decreased each time I woke, and even the food was bothersome, but I worried that if I ordered something outside of what was provided then I might not have enough to last until the next ship arrived.

Every morning a squeeze packet would be available in the dispensary, and every evening a grainy tofu-like jelly bar would appear, along with a packet of water that tasted like iron. The lavatory had a hole in the ground to squat over, and it would shoot a puff of air out to clean me when I finished, but not once had the door to the shower opened. My own stench was becoming too ripe for my own comfort.

Finally, I couldn't take it and pressed the button to speak with the A.I. in charge of the room to help, even if it cost me extra credits to use the shower.

"How may I assist you?"

"Can you open the door to the cleaning station?"

"All rooms in the Blue District are programmed to provide everything you need, no matter your species. My sensors do not see there is a need to use the lavatory station. You are still clean according to your species standards."

"I'm beginning to itch," I said in disagreement.

"This is considered a normal process of shedding dead skin," it said in a monotone disinterest that made me irritable.

"Are you going to let me use the cleaning chamber or what? Does that cost extra?"

The sound of the air suctioning through the vents startled me, before the computer replied, "I've sent your musk sample to our database for evaluation of your current care."

"What?" I squeaked. The warning given to me rang clear when I was given this room. Be careful what I agree to while in the Blue District, they will try to sell whatever they get access to. Now it seemed they had my scent saved up somewhere, like bottled ode de human.

"Open the lavatory!" I was done playing with the computer and wouldn't have them store up any more of my human musk.

"Thank you for choosing the Blue District for your safety and comfort," the computer chimed, and the door wheezed open, but not before I saw the credits on the account tick down. Fuck.

I peeled off my sweaty clothes but took them into the chamber with me as a mask dropped down. The mask clasped around my nose and mouth, including my eyes. The room filled up with powder, and my mouth heated from the cleaning light breaking apart any bacteria on my teeth. Warm wind blew through the space, and even though I knew I was clean, there was something very unsatisfying about not using water to rinse away the grime.

My clothes were still dusty from the wash when I stepped out, but the powder would absorb the oils and dirt before falling off.

Relief and panic filled me on the final day, I knew I'd wake up and the credits on my account would be zero. Was it the day I'd be collected and brought to the ship, or was it the day I'd be kicked out of this room and have nowhere to go? Still, there was no word from the ones who brokered my mating contract.

"Thank you for your stay at the Blue District," the computer spoke as I woke once more. "Please provide more credits to extend your stay or choose from a variety of services."

"Can you access when the next human transport comes into Trillume?"

"Of course. The next incoming trade ship with Earth was scheduled to arrive tomorrow, but due to disturbances with an anti-alliance terrorist group seeking to end H.E.T. services, the transport was delayed to protect the incoming contracts. All trade with Earth was suspended temporarily. Would you like to hear the latest news clips on the subject?"

"Yes!" I snapped.

This was bad. I was out of credits, and the longer I stayed here, the more likely it was my contract was in danger of being stolen by anyone seeking to take advantage. My contract was a liability now that it was no longer the original agreement. Anyone could claim that they were the ones that traded for rights to my contract since my alien mate took me here.

"Princess Klemon of Trillume has gone into hiding with her stance on humans deserving to be included in the Galactic Alliance. Many have taken the attack on Trillume transports as a sign of action to take control of the human beasts of Earth and seek to kill the princess to prevent any further disgrace with treating humans like anything more than a tradeable commodity, an exotic pet. Humans are an intriguing species that have increased in popularity, but there are restrictions on their contracts that are being debated in Central Trillume's Council."

The computer went on about the increase in activity within the Blue District concerning officials in Central Trillume. And here I was at the heart of it, and about to be released with no credits. With the unrest, caused by whatever incident was happening on Earth, I doubted the woman who brought me here would have an easy time returning here.

"You have a message. Would you like to accept it before you depart?"

Why wouldn't I?

"Yes...?"

"To the current resident of unit 4893," it was the voice of the woman who brought me here, "I have no way of reaching you without putting you in danger, and the ship you were meant to blend in with has been destroyed. The next transport isn't scheduled until next month. The Blue District is the safest place for you to be, but you can't stay in the room you're in now, since I've contacted you. You must survive until the next humans arrive on Trillume to hide your departure. Make your way to the Central District, if you can, to find a trill official to protect you. You can do it. I'll be sending a necia warrior to retrieve you in two days when your credits run out."

"But my credits are already gone now..."

"End of transmission."

"No, I'm out of credits! How am I supposed to wait for the warrior in two days? I'm not a secret agent capable of making my way to Central Trillume without help. I don't even know my way around! I'd get lost! I need credits." I nearly sobbed.

"You've expressed an interest in earning credits. Would you like to hear about our many services to earn credits here in the Blue District?"

I guess it wouldn't hurt to listen to what jobs were available here.

"Fine," I agreed with resignation.

"Thank you for your interest in making the Blue District a vital source of providing experiences for all species. Your species is classified as Earthling, subclass human. This species is gaining in curiosity and interest among many species across the galaxy. As such, the Blue District would happily accept your application to earn credits under our protection. Please proceed to a larger unit across the hall with a flashing gold light to accept earning credits here at the Blue District."

"Wait, what will I be required to do?"

I wasn't accepting anything without knowing what I was signing up for.

"You will be in control of what you provide for credits. Requests will be submitted by other guests for services from a human. You are in control of accepting or declining the service and its equivalent credit allowance. The room will be on the house for your first night while you establish your business. Do you agree?"

At least it was one night less to worry about while I wait for the necia warrior to come get me.

"I don't have to access any service requests?"

"You are not required to accept any requests, but should you not choose to accept at least one after your complimentary night for considering using the Blue District for your needs, then you will be asked to add credits to your account with us to continue your valued stay here. Do you accept?"

"I accept."

Chapter Four
Broma

"There are still concerns with human contracts. It will take more time before we're given any applicants from Earth while they sort through the trade concerns. Our contract is a bit different than the traditional one-earth year.

"Your mother made sure to include the addendum that states as long as you bond the human within that year, the contract becomes permanent and the human is thus under the rule of AsunGor laws," Romek explained when we arrived on Trillume.

"Permanency tends to frighten the humans, and an anti-alliance group has used our contract request as an excuse to attack in 'defense'. The original female your mother picked for you was killed, and you'll have to wait for new applicants for the contract."

"And you believe any female I'd pick next would not be harmed by this group of humans against trade contracts?"

"I didn't say they were all humans," he dismissed. "The group is a mix of all species against giving humans the rights to join the alliance. Your contract is more than giving a human the rights to breed with you. It is a high honor to be *the* delegate of *The* Commissioner of AsunGor. Your mother has left you with a pile of shit to clean up upon your arrival."

"We support the future leader of Trillume," Pheyal reminded Romek as he took a foreboding step forward. It seemed Romek had been on Trillume long enough to forget that he was indeed not a trill himself, and the old queen was known to take what she wanted without much diplomacy if diplomacy didn't match her wants. Princess Klemon was the future that kept our planet prosperous, and my mother knew that the price of keeping that loyalty strong would be to support her desire to have humans officially in the Galactic Alliance, and not simply a planet owned by the trill.

We were no different under the rule of the trill queen, and it was only because of our undesirable planet's surface that the unGor did well diplomatically. The trill disliked the harsh wind on their scales, and they disliked being underground.

"I have not forgotten," Romek growled back. "It was a warning that there will be some that would rather kill you than allow you to attend the next Council and throw your new title around with the intention of promoting humans."

"What do you suggest then?" Vaquel snapped with irritation.

He was even more invested in solving this than I was after he won the har fruit duel, but only after each of us failed equally many times and he was just more prepared with a scent neutralizer so he wasn't impaired in the next rounds. I still claim the results were cheating when both Pheyal and myself had more trouble avoiding bursting the sacks, distracted with the putrid scent.

"You should stay at the Blue District pods. They have the highest security on the planet, even better than the palace in Central Trillume. Not bad entertainment while you wait to claim your title and face the Council either."

"We will follow your advice," Pheyal agreed.

"No, not you," Romek objected, and Pheyal growled at him in response.

"Explain yourself," he said in warning.

"If we are seen together, it will be obvious that commissioner Broma is there. A couple of unGors together is normal, but a single unGor with more than one attendant, and one of your size is much too recognizable."

"I'll go," Vaquel stated.

"You will take me to the palace, where I will arrange the transfer of title for Commissioner Broma," Pheyal said pointedly to Romek, suspicion clear in his glare. He shifted his attention to me and gave a nod. "Do not go directly there. I'm not certain this isn't an attempt to separate us, and Romek may be bound to follow trill protocols without knowing who's pulling his ormete."

"I am not being pulled. I would have suggested going straight to the palace if I thought it was safe enough to do so," Romek objected. "In the storm, the clearest path is surrounded in dangers that you must not run from but take cover and let the storm pass."

"He even starts to sound like them," Vaquel said with distrust when we were out of earshot of both Pheyal and Romek. "Pheyal suspects that we'll be followed and Romek has the desire to take the title from you through your failure to adapt to Trillume, but he is still convinced he wouldn't resort to killing you."

"You do not share his thoughts," I suspected.

"He wouldn't risk killing you himself, but I wouldn't rule out using the anti-human group to do it for him."

"I memorized the map before we landed, and even if someone knows we're going to the Blue District, we just need to make it to the dome and we'd be under the protection of the district as long as we are paying customers," I assured him.

"You are not prepared for a duel without risking your ormete," Vaquel warned about not taking the threat seriously enough.

"I do not need to use my ormete to win a duel; it was simply a requirement when dueling for commission."

"Forgive me," he said with a bow of his head. I hadn't realized the threat in my tone towards him, and I sighed. There was still work to be done on keeping my tone diplomatic.

"I will remind you that outside of AsunGor, dueling is not about honor here. Even contracts are not kept without threat of consequences. It is why we do not use implants, as we do not trust the technology to not be tainted with the lure of power." Our language translators were external only. And easily disposed of. Which I took the time to unclip mine and toss it to the ground before my boot crushed the device to crumbs. Vaquel did the same with his and we disappeared into the crowd.

"Where do you think you're going?" We were cut off by the imposing figure of a large trill and a sickly appearing garrant beast with four arms and a strange rippling beneath its hide.

The garrant growled before adding, "Do you think the princess will send someone to help you?"

I lifted a brow at that turn of truth. This was less about my support, and more about luring out their primary target.

"You'll be coming with us," the trill said while grabbing Vaquel.

"I fear you'll be disappointed to know that Broma isn't officially appointed yet. Taking him won't be much of a threat to make Princess Klemon come out of hiding."

"What's he saying?" the garrant deferred to the trill.

"He's saying catching an egg before it is fertilized is but a small meal, while a hatched egg will be a larger feast," the trill explained in their typical manner of verbose analogies. "But what do we care about keeping the egg alive?"

The garrant grunted, obviously not in its right mind to realize the trill didn't care if Princess Klemon was lured out or not. It was telling of the trill's motives, and of the garrant's.

Vaquel eyed me, knowing what these fools were giving away the more they talked. And clearly understanding they were mistaking him for me. They were looking for a large unGor such as Pheyal with a normal sized unGor such as myself, but they weren't expecting that I wasn't that much smaller than Pheyal. Tacticians were a much more toned and compact build than a warrior, but he was still strong compared to other species. Vaquel was probably reveling being mistaken for the future Commissioner of all of AsunGor, given the smirk on his face, he was enjoying this.

"Killing me does you no good," he stated with the confidence of any honorable warrior of AsunGor. In more ways than one, his words were bringing him even more joy, knowing that even if he were to die, they earned nothing with the real Broma free to go.

I would not allow such a sacrifice, but he was earning my respect for the offer, nonetheless.

That alone would earn him the first claim on my mate's delegation celebration. He would be alive to see the day I'm bonded and seeking more support for my mate.

"Quiet!" the trill snapped.

"Dead bait doesn't earn a meal," the garrant rightly regained his wits enough to challenge the trill.

It was time for my interjection. "Might I suggest a compromise? Take him to the Blue District, place him in a room under your credit, and hold him hostage. I'm sure the supporters will wish to trade to make sure he can get back to the palace to claim his title."

"And you'd let us take him?" the trill seemed rightfully unconvinced.

"Of course not," I placated him. "I will follow you to the Blue District, and make sure you are placing him in a room by himself without the option of harm him in your care. It's also beneficial to you, as you wouldn't be safe stuck in a room with him. He's liable to sacrifice himself to kill you, that's how mad he's known to be. It is for your safety as much as his own."

Vaquel played into the role by growling his protest and snapping his jaw like a wild animal.

The trill's scales folded over each other at his forehead in disgust. "I have heard the rumors of his rise to commission. He sliced through his own flesh to harm his opponent, uncaring of whether he died as long as he was victorious."

That wasn't exactly how it went, I thought with amusement. It was strange how quickly and how exaggerated the stories became in such a short time.

"The only reason I have not killed you already is because I'm not uncivilized like your kind. If being your hostage means I get to have my title without murdering you, then that is preferable. But I'm not opposed to using you as an example like I have my own brother," Vaquel warned with a cool viciousness.

"If I wanted you dead, we wouldn't be talking at all," the trill ignored the threat, but the flutter in his scales on his head spoke of being uncomfortable with holding Vaquel so close.

"You could kill us here, but then you'd be killing more than us, wouldn't you?" I reasoned without flustering. It was true, their poison was deadly, but I had a feeling it drew too much attention, even for the Blue District, to poison an entire street. Their poison wasn't exactly subtle when it sprayed out of their scales like a mist.

"If you try anything, then it won't really matter if I cause a scene. Better to kill you all," the trill warned. He motioned for us to follow him as he tugged Vaquel along, turning his back to me. I could end them here, but there was no telling if they had backup groups ready to take up where these two left off. It was better to make it to the Blue District underground first.

I whispered to the garrant, who had extremely good hearing, "Guess he doesn't really value your life much, and whatever reason you need Broma alive for would be gone."

Before I could say more, the garrant was already charging without much thought. His mind was obviously under stress and his health was in serious question. Two fists smashed on either side of the trill's head and I could feel the crunch of the skull before he used his other arms to squeeze Vaquel.

"Sleep now," he said while Vaquel's eyes rolled back. He didn't even attempt to use his ormete to free himself. He was allowing himself to be caught at whatever cost, even his life, to make sure that I could go free.

The trill was left behind, but I wasn't sure if that would kill it when I'd seen them come back from worse. They were extraordinarily resilient.

We made it to the Blue District without further incident, and I did not provoke the garrant again with his unstable nature.

"You will stay back there. You can hear that I will give the computer instructions to keep the commissioner isolated," he gritted out barely containing himself.

"Agreed." I stayed back while he purchased his rooms and gave the isolation command. Even the one who purchased the isolation wasn't allowed to undo it until the contract term was up, so Vaquel would be safe for two risings.

"Now, you will give yourself an isolation command," he ordered while he shoved Vaquel's body into the transfer container reserved for unconscious guests.

"Of course," I said with a nod. I purchased my own unit and gave it an isolation command for two days, but with the contingency that the isolation was simply to the Blue District facility, not my room. But as this was a district designed for illegal trade, it was easy to fool the garrant.

"Isolation request complete," the computer intoned, and the garrant grunted his approval without having full faculties to confirm what kind of isolation was requested. It was mostly for the garrant to know that I would have no way of following him or trying to get help to free Vaquel. It was also helpful that privacy was respected here, and my name was never used to inform the garrant of his mistake.

"Wait." His large arms, all four of them, flexed as he watched me. Assessing me with scrutiny, he added, "Confirm isolation time."

"Please confirm my isolation time," I commanded the computer.

"One rising has been requested; please confirm duration," it stated.

"That is not what we agreed to! Two risings! It must be—"

"Of course," I interrupted, but kept my tone neutral and updated my time, "Adjust to two risings," I told the computer.

"Two risings confirmed, please proceed to your quarters through the right hall entry. Welcome to the Blue District. Enjoy your stay."

"Your stay has been confirmed. Please proceed to the left hall entry," the computer informed the garrant of his own stay confirmation. Before he departed, he warned, "I would consider a longer stay if I were you, as I don't need you alive, and I will kill you if I see you again."

I nodded my understanding and replied with a smile, "My sentiments exactly. Not even your friends care if you live, but I *do* care that you harmed him. If we meet again, I will kill you."

I didn't think Vaquel would grow on me so fast, but I didn't lie to the garrant. I would kill him if I saw him again for threatening those under my protection.

Walking down the hall of mostly rooms reserved for isolated chambers, it was an eerie feeling to not run into another guest of the Blue District while making my way to my room.

"Do you have no other guests on this floor?" I asked the computer running this establishment.

"Many are isolated on this floor, and the Blue District has many floors with two entrances to every room that connect to two different halls. I'm equipped to manage every guest according to their preferences for privacy. Many guests choose to wait until one of the two halls attached to their room is vacant before they depart, and there are separate floors for guests looking for experiences. Are you looking for company? We have the largest selection of species for various requests from scent stimulants to viewing rooms, or—"

"No, that will not be necessary. I'm waiting for a human mate."

"We have a human in residence, should you change your mind," the computer said, while an air vent above me opened and a soft puff blew down my ormete. It was a pleasant scent, but something in it made my muscles tense, like I should be alert for predators. It smelled like fear when a warrior faces their ormete ceremony to claim their first trophy. My hand instinctively lifted to touch the bone of my first kill. My ormete were still too weak to lift the weight of every memory. All I had left was my duty to find a human mate to keep peace for AsunGor.

"Male or female?" I asked the computer.

"It has not specified a gender for guests, but I can request permission to reveal this data? One request is complimentary for every guest."

It would be a waste of a request to ask such a simple question when I can get the same information with a different request.

"Request a time option with the human."

"Please specify the type of time option requested. No services are currently inventoried. It is their first rising open for guest interaction."

"I'll pay for a block on all other requests. The human will only be seen by me."

"Please confirm a single rising block on outside requests."

"Confirm," I said and watched as the screen on my wrist flashed the amount of an entire week of credits for one day of blocking requests on the human. "Robbery," I scoffed.

"Your request has been submitted to the human."

The light above my door turned blue, indicating 'occupied' to guests that might pass by my room. Inside, the space had basic accommodation, smaller than expected when I was used to spacious caverns. Even on my ship the crew quarters were larger than this, and it was a ship designed for speed, not cargo. We always made sure to utilize the limited cargo space for trade, but our ships were designed to be fast and sturdy to survive the winds of AsunGor's atmosphere.

The interface on the room's wall lit up with a notification.

"The human has added conditions to your request for time."

"State the conditions," I replied curiously.

"You are not allowed to gaze upon its form during your visit to its room. A sap will be applied to your eyes, which will naturally crack and fall off after a rising or once a dissolvent is applied. It wishes to remain what it calls "anonymous", which is defined as lacking a name in their tongue."

"You said conditions?"

"Yes, any requests during your time with the human are subject to denial at its discretion."

"I see..."

"You won't see; that is one of the terms," the computer corrected.

"I accept."

Regardless of what I found out about this human during my visit, at least I wouldn't be bored while I waited to rescue Vaquel. He'd be isolated for a couple risings, regardless of what I did, and I didn't need to find him, when I could easily ask the computer to lead me to him when his isolation was up, since the garrant did not specify that the guest was to be blocked from requests.

Vaquel was safe enough, and I'd get to meet my first human.

Chapter Five
Evie

I did it. I accepted a request. That should cover the time I was staying here for long enough to wait for the necia warrior to come get me, right?

"You have restricted the time request and added conditions. A warning has been given to the unGor about the fragility of humans; for your safety. Should you feel threatened by our guest, please use the extract code and the room will be fumigated with toxin to subdue all occupants. Blue Official District prides itself on being a safe place to pursue all pleasures in life. We thank you for choosing us to share your experiences."

"Uh, thank you," I paused thinking about how to address the computer running this place, "Blue Official District?"

"I detect discomfort, how may I assist?"

"Is that what I should call you?"

"Your species values names, a very trillian trait. The trill who frequent here call me BOD. It sounds different in trill tongue, but that would be the equivalent in your language."

"Bode..." That was oddly fitting for a place like this. Abode was a place to stay and bode was a predicted event. A place of predictable events of dubious nature, both the safest and most dangerous place on Trillume. Just accepting a request was a risk, but at least it was a calculated one with the protection of Bode.

"Are there any other requests for the day?" I asked Bode. I was expecting much more activity for a human when the news stated human contracts were suspended.

"Just the three provided. The third request included a clause to suspend requests until your time with them is completed."

"Oh." I wasn't sure what that meant to have someone pay to not allow other people to send requests to me, but it was clear from my credit balance that I wasn't paid for anything right away.

"I've sent your denial to the first request for observing your activities. The second request has been sent for and will arrive shortly. They have accepted your conditions to have their eyes covered in sap."

"Sap?"

"Yes, there is a krelin sap procured especially for sensory deprivation. It is a common request to blind guests."

I suppose I couldn't argue with that, considering I had asked for it myself.

"Right," I said mostly to hype myself up for what I was agreeing to.

The room was much bigger than what I was in before, and a door from behind me wheezed open as the suction of the airlock released. I whirled around, thankful that they were blinded and unable to see my shock.

Ter-ak?

The hood of his robes was down, and he sniffed the air as the door closed behind him.

I said nothing.

"It is you," he said finally, "Little viper. I can smell you."

I backed up and stumbled over the edge of the large bed, making me scramble back on the bedding.

"You—you—" I stuttered.

"Having a human mate is a diplomatic disadvantage if I wished to keep my position at the palace. I've been waiting for you to stop hiding, so we may return to my den. BOD has told me that I'm the first accepted request, and it is time we leave before you're damaged by the kind of beings that frequent the Blue District."

"You sold me," I stuttered, barely above a whisper.

"It was necessary," he dismissed.

"You said I was a demon," I said while backing away. He thought I was more interested in books than preparing food together, which was apparently a big deal for trill intimacy. If I was given a bit more time, I would have found that out eventually and made more of an effort to help.

"Is that not what your kind calls beings that are fierce in their activities? Your face was deeply captivated by the tablet of tomes. To seek one source is to know nothing, but a moon set as another rises," he spoke in a trill proverb at the end that gave me pause. He was waiting for me to understand his words, and I sighed.

"You're saying there are more ways to seek knowledge than from books. Are you saying you wanted me to ask you?"

"Is that not what being mated means? To rely on one another?"

He could have said that—before he sold my contract. Ter-ak took a slow step closer, like stalking a frightened animal. My back pressed against the wall, reaching the limit of how far I could get away without changing directions.

The spikes on his head flexed, and a spray misted in the room. Fuck, that was something I read about. Was he trying to poison me? The trill were capable of killing their prey by spraying them.

"What did you do?" I squeaked.

"This is how a trill mates. I should have done this sooner to bond us appropriately. You are inhaling my poison, and my mark will mean my poison will never harm you." He smiled, showing off a row of razor-sharp teeth.

I pressed my lips together, hoping I didn't inhale too much, but knowing all it took was one whiff. It was mate with him or die...

"No," I mumbled through my fingers as I covered a gasp. The sound of the vents spinning to life and a beeping distracted me from keeping my eyes on Ter-ak.

"Violation detected," BOD, the AI of the Blue District, spoke. "Trill poison is prohibited on the premises. Incompatible with Earthlings. If the human is harmed, your account will be charged for the inconvenience, and you will be required to fight for your freedom in the arena against our champion. Air filtering in process, a bounty has been issued to nearby guests to ensure your cooperation."

"Cancel bounty and violation," Ter-ak ordered BOD without any change to his tone. He was unworried about the reaction the AI was giving. "Command override initiated, clearance in accordance with trill mating rights of palace officials. This human is my mate, and my poison will not harm her once I mark her."

"Trill mating rituals accepted, contract confirmed with your ID. Please proceed to mark your mate before the poison can harm the Earthling."

"No," I objected, but my voice was nothing more than a gasp as I felt my knees give way, my back sliding down the wall.

Ter-ak towered over me, his tail grazed the floor, closing in toward my feet. This wasn't how I imagined bonding with an alien mate, and I closed my eyes, not wanting to accept it, but knowing what was coming.

His tail lifted my chin up, and I opened my eyes to him glaring at me, having removed the resin from his eyes. "Look at me when I give you my mark. Mates are not prey, human; they face their bonded."

Then I watched in horror as blood poured out of his mouth. Ter-ak's throat had grey ropes wrapped around it with sharp bones piercing into his soft flesh not covered by scales.

"Where I come from," a deep voice whispered, "a female has the right to kill anyone who tries to force their way into her delegation."

"Bounty fulfilled," BOD's announcement echoed in my mind. "Please insert both female and trill into the lav station for health scans."

Ter-ak's body was tossed to the side, and a large grey alien sniffed the air and then crouched down, cocking his head to the side as if listening for my breathing. His eyes were covered in a black sap that looked like plastic wax. His silvery grey hair was braided in ropes that fell over his shoulder, adorned with sharp bones, carved into unique shapes. He had a bone pierced through his ear pointed towards me.

"I don't smell blood from you, but it is best to be safe and have you scanned by the AI," he said while offering me his hand.

"Ter-ak?"

"If that is the trill's name, then he should be fine after he hibernates. They are a rather resilient species. I do apologize if you had wanted to mate with him. I had fully intended on being your only suitor, but the AI had told me while I was on my way that you were in need of assistance. To my surprise the bounty was the same room I was heading to. Shall we?"

It was strange hearing the translation in my implant sound so formal when his voice was deep and throaty.

"Thank you," I whispered and watched as a shiver started in his offered hand and seemed to travel up to his shoulder, making him stretch out his neck.

"What a pleasant sound you make," he admitted when my hand slipped into his. I blushed; not that he could see that. "Are you able to lead me to where the lav station is? I can request our host to dissolve the sap from my eyes, but I fear I'd be in breach of contract and another bounty will be sent for me this time."

"Oh," I tried to scramble from the floor, but my legs were heavy and I tumbled into his arms. "Sorry." I tried to push away, but his arms wrapped around me as his chin rubbed through my hair. He breathed in deeply with a groan, before swooping me up to carry me.

"You can be my eyes, and I can be your legs," he said while I felt his chest puff out a bit under his cloak.

"Behind you," I whispered. "The lav station. Y-you take five steps to the right and it's beside the bed." Right, he couldn't see the bed, or anything. I was about to explain further, but noticed his steps were much larger than mine, and I had to squeak for him to stop. I needed to do it one step at a time. "You have to open the door first. Here, let me." I unwrapped one arm from around his neck to press my hand on the scanner to open the door.

The lav station was open, and with one step at a time, the large alien placed me gently inside. The door slid shut around me, lasers scanned over me, and something shot out to pricked me on the back of my arm.

"Hey?" I clipped as I rubbed my arm.

"Trill poison detected. Please retrieve the trill for antidote," BOD requested.

I heard the alien grunt outside the lav station. "There are two ways to cure trill poisoning. Take the mate mark, or drink their venom. The mate mark is simply a way of retrieving the venom. Which do you prefer?" he asked me.

"I can just drink venom and be cured?" Then I remembered that he couldn't see. "But your eyes?"

"I can easily find the trill by his blood. It will be my honor to prove my usefulness, little mate."

"Mate?" I squeaked, but he was already gone to retrieve the venom.

Chapter Six
Broma

My skin hummed just thinking about the little human's touch along my ormete as she clung to my neck. A smile plastered on my face as I felt the trill's teeth scrape across my hand as I dug into its mouth, searching for the venom sack. At the roof of its mouth, I felt one of them had already been depleted in preparation for mating. Carefully, I extracted the hardened capsul with a sharpened nail claw. I'd give it to my little mate first. Normally, a warrior would simply pop the sack into their mouth and consume it, but perhaps the AI here could synthesize a few antidotes from one sack. My nose crinkled at what I would have to do if the AI couldn't. The other venom sack was dispersed in his teeth to mark a mate. If I had to be marked by that trill, I would kill him before he could ever claim to be my mate.

Returning to the lav station, I lifted the hardened sack in my palm, and a mechanical tube suctioned it up.

"You're hurt," her beautiful sound translated into the ear-piece I wore.

"It will heal," I assured her. "Is it enough?" I asked the AI.

"The Earthling is small and requires little. Recovery should be quick. Due to your size, I'll inject the remaining amount directly to the source contact in your hand. It should be sufficient, given the quick application."

My shoulders relaxed at the relief of not having to be mated to the trill even if for a temporary amount of time.

"Excellent," I replied before using my mate's scent to calm myself. Something to focus on besides the ache in my ormete. It was ill-advised to use them so soon after their reattachment, but I'd do it again knowing another was forcefully claiming her.

Then I heard her soft dysregulated breathing catching in her throat, before she seemed to hold her air like her airways were restricted. I paused, my hand reaching out in her direction as I crouched.

"Are you afraid of me?" I questioned, as that was the best outcome of such circumstances, better than the thought that her small body was struggling with the antidote and that fluttering heartbeat would cease. Perhaps the Earthlings were not strong enough to mate with a trill and I had come seconds too late to save her...

Not being able to see her was torture, and I was near ready to tear my own flesh to remove the sap from my eyes when her breath gasped and a soft hand touched mine. A rumbling grew in my chest and she retreated, but her fingertips still touched like she could feel the same pull in her ormete that I did. Earthlings did not have control over their ormete like an unGor, but perhaps that was an unconscious choice in their evolution.

"Why isn't the AI healing your hand?"

"It knows my species does not appreciate losing a memory by healing a scar. Every mark is a map of my life, a life well lived that may be recounted by those who come after me."

She whimpers. "Are you dying?"

I chuckled. A sound I wasn't accustomed to before meeting my brothers Pheyal and Vaquel, and it seemed this small female could be another to see a smile not of diplomacy, but something deeper. She cared for my well-being despite her circumstances.

Then I felt her soft finger jab at my tender wound in my hand as a stifled sob clutched her throat again. It was not the wound that ached the most, though I should have been more concerned about the trill's poison than I was.

"It isn't funny," she mumbled.

"Of course, Little Delegate. My apologies. I will not die from this, it is the way of the unGor clans to appreciate every wound that can remind us of powerful moments in our lives. If there was not a wound, I would wish to create one that could do our meeting justice."

"Some wounds are never seen; do you create one for those?" she asked with a hollowness that stung deep in my gut. It was as if she were not speaking to me at all but of something inside her that could not be seen on the delicate surface of her skin.

"Who has harmed you?" I did my best to steady my tone, but I was uncertain how my voice would be heard by an Earthling with her sound so soft and quiet. My hand wrapped around her small one, holding it as gently as I could.

She sighed, and I wished the sap would fall from my eyes to see her.

She chuckled with a hiccup. "The universe..."

"That is a very large duel you've claimed for yourself," I soften my voice so it doesn't startle her. To battle the universe is the one duel that lasts a lifetime and cannot be done alone. My commissioner, as tender as my mother has ever been to me or my brothers, would say it is foolish to think one unGor can defeat every obstacle without delegating to those they can trust. This is why our mates are called delegates. They share the burden of our hearts and help ease the heaviness of life's trials. "You must choose wisely on who you trust to help you defend against such a vast and ongoing duel."

I wished to include that I could be a wise choice, but that was not how I was taught to be chosen by a delegate. It is proven with action, not words. Words were earned and I have not earned the right to say them to her.

"Am I supposed to trust you?" she whispered so low, I almost missed it.

I smiled. "Only after I've proven myself."

There was a silence between us that was only filled with the way one of her fingers rubbed against my hand holding hers. An electric current seemed to generate from the contact that I felt stir my carnal desires and fill my body with heat.

"How does an unGor prove themselves?"

"We provide trophies of our ability to protect them from dangers; this wound will be my first earned trophy in your honor. One rising, you may choose to add an adornment to my ormete braid to accept my offerings. Other offerings may be displays of my skills that may prove useful to you."

I felt the air shift as her breath heated on my chest. I could smell her scent begging me to lean in closer. Another hand reached out to touch my ormete strands and I felt a shiver tremble through them, jolting my cock to life.

"Is that what these are? Your past trophies?"

A rumble vibrated through my chest before I controlled myself to keep still.

"My past accomplishments mean nothing by my mouth; they must be heard by others for them to earn me any respect."

"And do they?" her voice deepened, and I couldn't help the way my ormete heated at her touch; she would likely be seeing the way the strands glow when excited. My ormete was silver, much like the rocks of AsunGor. Would she find it attractive? My brother Brakaun had more desirable black ormete with fine skin the color of the sands on the surface, instead of the grey coloring of the caves. What made me effective at blending in with predators was also a disadvantage, with females looking to be reminded of the beauty beyond the domes.

"Not presently," I try to keep the gravel of lust from my words. Without her knowing the stories then my trophies mean nothing.

"What did you come here for?" she asked while her fingers stroked across my ormete. I groaned, unable to stop it from lifting up my throat. I regretted it immediately as her fingers stopped moving, retreating from me.

"I am to claim a title from the palace as a diplomat of Asun-Gor, and return with a mate to further my planet's relations with Trillume."

Perhaps she will accept being my delegate and I can court her properly, but the way her hand twitched in my hold told me that returning to my planet probably reminded her of being forced to mate with me as the trill had tried to do. "I will not harm you," I assured.

"Right..." she sighed before she whispered, "I'm sorry." Then she tried to extract her hand from mine, and I did not wish for our contact to be forced so I eased my hold, feeling her slip through my fingers.

Chapter Seven
Evie

He was here to find a trill mate, and I'd been responsible for him killing a trill diplomat.

My lower jaw trembled at what it would mean for both of us to be found with Ter-ak's body. The palace would be furious.

"Will they punish you for harming Ter-ak?" I held my body to comfort myself, the chill from fighting off the poison still coursing through my veins. It was selfish, but I knew whatever they would do to punish him would be much worse for me and I needed to know if I would die because of this.

"Ter-ak? Is that his name? I had not expected him to have given you his name. That was presumptuous of me. I believe I've heard his name as one of the trill I was supposed to meet with at the palace later. If he is wise, he will not wish to mention this incident when we meet again. You are the only one who needs to know what this scar will remember for us. If he decides differently, all it does is add to my reputation."

I breathed a sigh of relief. Ter-ak wasn't dead; not if he was still speaking of him as if he would see him again. But then a chill traveled up my spin.

"Will he..." I couldn't bring myself to ask what would happen when he wakes.

"Wake again? Yes, the trill are a resilient species. They hibernate and come back time and time again from near death instances. I could sever his head to make sure he doesn't heal, if you are afraid of him?"

"No," I squeaked.

"That is a relief. It would be more difficult to bargain with the palace after knowing I have killed a diplomat of theirs, though I am under no obligation to disclose my actions while in the Blue District."

"You mean to bargain for a mate," I mumbled, feeling oddly jealous of another woman that would have a better match than the one I found lying in the other room. I wasn't a diplomat, or even under the protection of my contract anymore.

"Among other things," he agreed. "The trill are very attached to their contracts, and they have many resources, including control over Earthling trade and customs. It is rare to find a human outside trill protection."

"Me," I gasped, wondering if I should be backing away from this large, yet strangely alluring alien. His hair had braids that glowed silver, and skin that looked like granite rock that twinkled in the light. It would have been nice to see his eyes, since his voice was even and deep. I didn't really know what was going on in his head.

"Is there another?" he teased, and my worries evaporated.

A boldness came over me as I leaned in once more to whisper, "What kind of skills will you show your mate to earn her approval?"

There was something empowering about knowing he couldn't see me, and if he tried to hurt me the AI, BOD, would send a contract out to kill him.

"Is that an invitation?" His normally even voice vibrated with a growl that made me shiver. Fuck, he was so attractive, and the adrenaline of nearly being forced to mate with someone by poisoning was heightening my fear of knowing I may die tomorrow with regrets. The Blue District was about having experiences and yet he was still asking for my permission. My body heated all over and I absently stroked his jaw line with my free hand.

"Show me," I pleaded quietly. *Show me what it means to be a cherished mate. Show me what it means to earned, not taken.*

The strands of his hair floated in the air, and I gasped as one braid gently stroked across the back of my hand that held his cheek. Glowing silver, his hair twined around my wrist, tugging at me to come closer. And I silently obeyed, crawling into his lap, where his arms wrapped around me and lifted me up.

I stared at his features around the black sap molded to his eyes. There were fine grey lines, one darker on his chin that despite the smoothness of his skin, made me think these were scars as I ran my finger over the larger one in particular.

"Will you tell me about them?"

"Once I've earned the right to boast and have removed the fear that my failures would tarnish your thoughts."

I stifled a giggle at the ridiculousness of this large man being afraid of anything after easily taking down a trill like Ter-ak.

We stood at the sliding door out of the lavatory when he chuffed. *Oh, right*, I thought, at realizing he couldn't see anything. I pressed my hand to the wall, and the door slid open, but it wasn't to the room. The hallway was clear and I saw that this was actually a second entrance to the room.

"A new room has been procured; please proceed to the end of the hall where your scent can be masked before continuing," BOD addressed through the intercom.

"To your right," I whispered, seeing the floor light up towards what appeared to be an elevator.

Instead, he took a left. "The right," I repeated and tapped his shoulder in the direction.

"You have no reason to hide your scent when with me. Only others in isolation are allowed on my floor. Anyone looking for you will not be able to find you if you allow me to take you. Tell the AI that you will join my isolation unit." He paused and sighed at my hesitation. "I will not force you. You may follow the AI to the room provided and I will submit a new request to see you."

He started to lower me to the ground, and my arms tightened around his neck. I didn't want to let him go. I nodded into his chest.

"Under Blue District bylaws, you will be required to purchase the human's contract with the facility. Do you accept the terms?"

When he didn't answer, I waited until he whispered into my hair, "The AI is asking for your permission to end your contract with them, and I will be responsible for paying the credits to sever the contract. Trillume is full of contract law, but you have not entered any contract with me by agreeing to sever the Blue District's right-to-work contract."

"I agree," I squeaked.

"Understood. Proceed to the isolation units on the next floor."

But the elevator was on the other side, wasn't it? One of the doors that looked like any other room opened and led to another hallway with more room doors. He stopped, and I watched as his hair seemed to lift like an invisible breeze controlled it. Then he turned and walked down the hall but stopped again when another door opened to an elevator. The whole facility was like a maze; any of the doors could have been a room, another hallway, or an elevator. They all looked the same on the outside, aside from the light above the door that was red, blue, or gold. The same blue light glowed along recessed under lighting, and every door looked like any other.

My finger kept tracing the black design on his shoulder, wondering what this scar represented for him. It seemed to avoid the muscle that flexed as he held me in his arms.

"Every unGor saves that spot for their mate to mark. It is a bad omen for our species to scar that area before mating."

"Oh," I gasped and snapped my finger back, not realizing I was doing something offensive to his species. I wasn't his mate, after all.

He wasn't in the Blue District to find a mate, I thought logically. He was a diplomat looking for a trill mate, not a human.

"I will procure the proper contracts for mating and return to AsunGor for the delegate ceremony," he explained, and this tightness in my chest clamped down.

"Of course," I said absently with a nod. My contract was traded with a necia warrior waiting for me to make the next ship off Trillume.

"Can you tell me about the unGor?" I added after an awkward silence. Not that the knowledge would help me with what my future held, but it didn't hurt to pretend for a night.

"A diplomatic answer would be to say we are excellent strategists and have valuable resources that many species have use for, but most of all, our ships are faster than even the best trill enforcers."

"And the nondiplomatic?" I asked curiously.

"Many unGors are used as bounty hunters, and though necia are known as the warriors of the Trillume Galaxy, the unGor are the enforcers of diplomacy due to our unmatched speed in both our ships and our skills."

"That's how you snuck up on Ter-ak," I mused. He was able to do all that while blinded by sap. It was impressive, and yet he moved so purposefully through the hallways. Each step was so measured and smooth; if I were watching from behind him, I wouldn't have guessed he couldn't see. Secretly, as we rode up in the elevator, I stuck my tongue out at him. His braids twitched, but I couldn't be certain it was related.

"Have your airways been obstructed from the poison?" he questioned with urgency as his arms squeezed a bit tighter around me.

I wheezed from his hold, slightly coughing on my own words, "No. I stuck my tongue out at you."

"Great moons," he growled and eased his hold on me while rolling his shoulders to ease the tension built up in his muscles.

Curious on if he could actually see me, I stuck my tongue out again, and this time he stopped breathing. The door opened on the elevator, but he remained still as a rock. He could have been mistaken for a statue.

"Tell me." He finally said with forced measure, "BOD, did she display her tongue to me again?"

"I'm right here," I pouted at him asking the AI.

"Confirmed," BOD replied. "The human has displayed her tongue to you twice now."

"According to the treaty agreement between AsunGor and Trillume, section ninety—" he stopped, like he was thinking of which article he was referring to but couldn't remember.

"Tongue displays are referenced in your treaty?" I wondered out loud.

"You are within your rights to pursue section ninety under the article of engagement only after the human displays a third time, due to her classification not being recognized by the Trillume Council."

"Understood," he said. His hair caressed my chin as if he could see through the black sap across his eyes. "I don't have to see to hear the subtle sound of your lips opening for me, or the way your pulse increases across your delicate skin where we touch. Display your tongue again, and I will show you what I can do with mine."

I gulped, and absently, my tongue flicked to lick my lips. A boldness came over me, knowing he couldn't see. To make sure he knew I was displaying my tongue in whatever strange ritual that meant for an unGor, I leaned in and licked his neck. His chest rumbled and wind swept up under my hair as he sped down the hall and entered an open room door. It closed behind us, and blinked blue before the room descended into darkness around us. I couldn't even see the tip of my nose, until his hair glowed like sparkling stars.

His head nuzzled into my neck and his tongue's warmth heated my skin from my clavicle to behind my ear, making me shiver.

"Tell me to stop," he whispered in my ear, but I couldn't bring myself to say the words.

"Tell me you don't want me to touch you," he added as he lowered me to the bed, my head resting on his injured arm, yet he made no complaint. His other hand trailed down my arm, a finger gently stroking the inside of my elbow. I shivered, a soft moan escaping my lips.

This moment was ours, private, and for tonight... he was mine.

"Touch me," I whimpered, guiding his hand lower. He stopped at my waistband and rubbed my lower back, before he let his other arm slip out from under my head. His tongue trailed between my breasts before kissing just under my swell with a softness that drove me crazy, near begging for more pressure. What was he doing to me? My thighs squeezed together, but he rotated me with my cheek planted on the cushions of the bed and his breath heavy on the small of my back. The material of my shirt ripped up, exposing my back to him. Warmth gathered where his tongue trailed, and his hair tickled like little fingers massaging everywhere. His hands roamed my sides up to rub his thumbs at the side of my breasts then back down again, memorizing my shape as he caressed me.

For the first time in my life, I moaned at having my body touched like it was a place of worship. My fingers itched to touch him. I reached out to return the feeling to him, but instead he grabbed my hand, guiding it back to myself. He didn't worship me for reciprocation and that confused me further as my own fingers touched my skin with his fingers atop them, giving gentle nudges for me to continue. The material of my pants was becoming too much to bear. I needed more.

Then he kissed at the crest of my ass, and I moved my hand beneath my waistband to tug it down. He groaned and swiftly pulled them free before his tongue was on my skin once more. My hips lifted, to give him better access to my soaked panties. He sniffed the material, and sucked it up into his mouth, making me gasp as my clit was gathered up in the same action. I pulled the material to the side and throbbed as his tongue swiped between my lips.

The intense desire to be filled made my thighs clench around his head and felt the way his hair caressed my legs as my hips lifted to bring him closer. His hands gripped my ass and pulled me down the bed to get better access. I wanted to scream out his name, but I didn't even know what to call him.

I gasped as something pushed at my entrance. His fingers gripped my hips and rubbed into my ass, so it couldn't be his hands.

Panting out my confusion, I was about to ask when I sucked in my words from the way my pussy clenched around the warm pressure. It wasn't his tongue, because that was working against my clit, playfully sucking and burying his nose and chin up and down my sensitive flesh. Whatever it was curled up and vibrated against my inner walls.

My— "God!" I dug my nails into his shoulders and convulsed at the sudden waves of sensations ripping through me. I'd never felt like this with anyone before. It had always taken so long to work up to an orgasm, but it was like he knew exactly where to go and how much touch to give to set me off.

"Broma," he corrected as he nuzzled between my legs and licked his lips.

"What was that?" I rocked myself against his cheek as I came down from the way my muscles twitched without my input.

"I followed where your blood was most active; that is usually a sign of where the most sensitive areas are. On AsunGor, we have exceptional hearing and are able to track in the dark beneath the surface. There is a fruit that grows at the roots whose juice we practice extracting without disturbing their defensive mechanisms. You are sweeter than any har fruit."

I had no idea what a har fruit was, but if that was what he thought I tasted like, I'd be curious to try one someday. What was AsunGor like? He said he'd return there after he finished claiming his title and a mate.

As he pulled back more, I watched as his hair uncurled from between my legs.

"It was your hair?"

"My ormete," he corrected.

"Ormete," I repeated, staring at the way they glowed in the dim light of the room. "It's warm," I said while part of the braid caressed my thigh.

"They fuse together to become stronger. Our ormete do not unravel once they bond."

They looked like dreadlocks, but as I watched the glow of the strands, it was like veins pulsing. Some strands were not bonded towards the top of his head, and some stray ormete strands were shorter and lifted free of the braids. There were bones laced through the thick strands, and the twisted lock that pet between my legs appeared without any adornments, slick with my pleasure

"It's beautiful," I said while reaching to touch the one with a strange sickle-like bone at the end. It didn't glow quite like the others half of the fused locks didn't lift to greet me like the one slipping closer to my entrance again. "Can you feel them?"

"Only when the blood pumps into them," he seemed to hesitate, like he was thinking of what to say, or leaving something out, "Can you feel yours?" He asked about the hair between my thighs where he nuzzled his nose into. I giggled before wiggling my hips, but his hands kept me in place.

"No, but I'd feel it if the root is pulled."

"I do not sense any blood in your ormete."

"It's a protein, not connected to blood."

"It connects somewhere, or it would not have grown. If my ormete was not connected, then it would not be able to do this," he teased as his smooth rope of hair, like a tentacle, slipped between my lips. It pushed at my entrance, staying at the edge just on the cusp of filling me, but holding back to trace circles where my body clenched on emptiness.

"Mmm," I moaned as the tension built, he pulsed at my core, not going farther, coming so close to giving me what I wanted, but not retreating as he slipped over where I ached for him in a tantalizing dance to drive me crazy.

"I could listen to that forever," he said with a groan.

Thinking of forever made me shiver. It was a false sentiment I'd heard before, but for a moment I wanted to believe it.

"What would forever look like?" I asked as I rocked against the way he edged the pleasure building in my core. After the words came out of my mouth I immediately regretted them.

This wasn't the time to speak about forever and I had to remind myself that it was okay to live in the now, without a thought of the future. I squirmed against the way his tentacle rubbed around, then pushed at my entrance, teasing me.

All of my common sense, future, and past evaporated as my present need grew.

I hadn't expected an answer, but he pulled back, making me whine in protest. His tentacle lifted to his mouth and he licked my juices before he moaned his own approval of my taste.

"Forever is by my side," he said while sucking my juices from his ormete tentacles. "Change the minds of the council with the success of AsunGor. Building a new commission, and seeing the smile of my bonded, my delegate, full of everything I can give."

"What will you give me?" I panted, feeling an ache in my chest at how I wasn't who he was seeking to be his bonded, but some trill he'd find after we were done.

"Everything," he said while leaning down on his arms to brush his nose against mine, seeking out my lips.

An overwhelming need to bring him closer to me took over, my arms wrapped around his neck and pulled him down. I squeezed tightly not wanting to let him go. My skin heated where we connected and my hips lifted, wanting him to melt within me.

I was starved to feel wanted, and every touch he gave made me want more.

Our lips met and he held me as tightly as I clung to him. Through ragged breaths, I moaned as my body heated and my skin became tender; his hand sizzled down along my side and around my thigh. He clutched and tugged, lifting my leg and opening myself to him fully.

I gasped as pressure built at my entrance, then his large cock slipped up and through my lips, rubbing across my clit. Shivering, I rubbed myself against him. There were ridges towards the top that were soft but hard, creating the perfect combination to make me squirm. My hips bucked up as his cock notched within me. We both stilled. I opened my eyes to see the veins of his tentacles glowing. It was warm and made my stomach ache to keep this feeling. His cock throbbed within me as he waited for me to adjust to his fullness.

Embarrassed, I buried my face into his shoulder and nuzzled in, holding him close. He grunted as I moaned with surprise that he wasn't fully seated, but I felt him pushing deeper until I felt him touch something inside of me that made my limbs weak. It was only a moment to regain myself, but then he pulled back and thrust back to tap that spot again, and I spasmed.

His hips rocked, rubbing at that tender sensation so deep that I never knew it existed before now. My hips sought out for more, while equally retreating from being overwhelmed. He held on to my ass to keep me in place. Unable to control my own body, he helped me move to keep the pressure building until I screamed with my nails digging into his back. My walls clutched around his cock, seeking to milk him of his essence.

A tingling sensation was warming through my stomach and moving down into my toes and out to my fingertips.

"What is that?" I gasped as my body turned to jelly and I became very sleepy. No, no, no. Don't go to sleep. I tried to hold on, but then my arms went limp.

Chapter Eight
Broma

What have I done? I brushed the hair away from her cheek and behind her ear. Her ormete was lifeless as she slept, but it seemed to glow as I touched it.

"We are bonded, My Delegate," I whispered and kissed the top of her ear.

The bond is only beginning. My mate will need to allow me to give more of myself before the bond becomes permanent. As soon as we leave this place, I'll have the contract made official with the council. According to my own customs we were already mated, but without more contact, the bond will fade without being nurtured.

Her face was soft in her sleep as she accepted our bond within her body. *You'll sleep less the more our bond grows*, I think as if she could hear my thoughts. My fingers prodded at the sap stuck to my eyes. I could scrap it off, but it would surely take some skin along with it. I wanted nothing more than to see my mate, but feeling her would have to be enough for now.

"I do not wish to leave you, but I must find Vaquel. I will return."

Grabbing my robe from the floor, I winced at the sting of the fabric brushing against my ormete. In the moment, I had forgotten how tender they were from battling with them earlier against the trill. I licked my lips, still tasting my mate on my tongue. It was easy to get lost within her. She eased all of my pains, but I could feel the poison from the trill was slow to heal with the antidote. Mating was only a temporary reprieve from the ache.

"There is currently a guest in the main hall, would you like to use the secondary hall?" the AI suggested.

"No need. A guest would hardly be threatened by a blinded unGor." Though, they would be if they knew how often we hunted without light to guide our eyes.

"As you request," they said as the door whirred open. "The guest has opted to remain in the hall."

Interesting.

"Searching for something?" I asked as I stepped out. The door closed behind me to protect my mate.

"You smell of mating. It seems I had nothing to worry about," Romek's voice was heard down the hall.

"Romek..." What was he doing in the isolation chambers? Only guests requesting isolation were in these halls. Something didn't sit right with me and all I could think was the Blue District BOD AI had only said there was one guest in the hall, and I'd left Pheyal with him. "Where's Pheyal?"

"He was held up at the palace to secure your title, but we were worried when we didn't hear from you. I thought you would choose an isolation chamber to prevent others from the anti-alliance from group finding you."

It made sense, but my ormete buzzed with adrenaline, like I should be alert to predators. My lack of sight could be a contributor to that, but I had to be sure.

"I need to secure a contract with my mate as soon as possible," I changed the subject. He should be asking where Vaquel is, if he is truly concerned.

"Absolutely," Romek agreed. "I'll have the contract prepared. You can add your mate when we return to the palace." He hesitated before adding, "The council will be pleased you've found a mate so quickly, but we should make sure the contracts are prepared at the palace and not connected with the Blue District."

He still hasn't asked of Vaquel...

"Vaquel will be worried," I prompted.

"In the eye of the goddess, they who neglect their duty are forgotten," he shook his head in disgust, "It is disgraceful that he is not at your side. I should have been the one to join you."

Romek did not give any indication that he knew Vaquel was taken, but I did not like the way he sounded more trill than unGor, even in my presence. If I could see his expression, I could make more observations to whether he knew more, but as it was, I had to trust he was here because he was smart to know I'd be in isolation.

"Come, come. We must wait out the night and return to the palace as soon as the isolation ends."

Without realizing it, I was putting distance between me and my room where my mate rested. The attack from the garrant and the trill had me distrusting everything.

But I put on a diplomatic smile and nodded. "Let us return to your chamber."

"And your mate?"

"She'll be resting for a while yet; best not to disturb her."

"How fortunate to find a strong bond," he replied in a strange tone devoid of emotion. Was that jealousy?

Guided by the sound of the door opening, and the soft beeping of the AI allowed me to easily navigate the hall. Once I arrived where the sound was echoing loudest, the door closed on what I assumed was the elevator. I wouldn't be able to leave the

Blue District, but my isolation was not limited to the isolation rooms. Though, if Romek was able to enter my floor, he also had an isolation unit. Did he volunteer to be isolated in an attempt to find me after losing contact?

"There are many floors for isolation," he sensed my curiosity.

Why was he on my floor, then?

"Here we are," he said as a door opened to a blood-curdling howl that set my ears on fire.

Romek pushed me to the side, and I wondered if that was to protect me from whatever was making that screeching noise. The door closed behind us.

"The guest is in distress," BOD explained as I was sprawled on the floor, my ormete tingling with my own distress at feeling a presence of danger.

"What has happened?" Romek demanded.

The smell of blood was pungent in the air, and I braced myself for what I couldn't see.

"Sedatives are ineffective, and the guest is not coherent in thought."

The screams echoed, and I heard the distinct sound of flesh being torn apart, and something wet and sticky slapped against my arm. I carefully picked the thick slab from my flesh, and my nostrils flared.

"Remove my sap, immediately," I snapped at the AI.

A mist sprayed on my face, and the sap melted, dripping from my eyes. I waited for the weight of the substance to lift, and I opened my eyes to the horror before me.

The garrant from earlier was flailing on the ground, tearing its own skin off. Gashes and flesh scattered around him as he rolled in pain. Romek rushed to hold him down.

"What is he doing here?" I glared at Romek.

"He was demanding a ransom for holding you captive, and I thought it would be fitting to show up and interrogate him with the very one he claimed to have at my side."

Again, his explanation made sense but didn't sit right with me.

"Why aren't the sedatives working on him?" I asked BOD.

"I'm analyzing the blood," there was a pause before a steel reinforcement slammed down over the door behind me, "Warning. Warning. Anomaly detected. Here, at the Blue District, I pride myself on maintaining a safe place for all species. You will remain isolated until the anomaly is resolved."

"What anomaly?" I asked as the garrant twitched and stopped moving.

"You have been exposed to the remains of an unknown death of a guest. Until it is determined you are not the cause, and that you pose no threat to the rest of the guests, you will remain in this room."

"Stubborn species," Romek muttered to himself.

"You know what this is," I said with no reservations now that I could see the way he was unconcerned with the amount of blood splattered on him during the garrant's struggle.

"So do you," he wiped his hands on his robes before continuing, "You'll understand when you take a closer look."

I approached and saw the purple scales underneath the deep gashes. "The solungors..."

The virus was supposed to have been eradicated.

"The garrants are notorious for faking their medical records. They are suspicious of all things not made from their own planet. I was hoping we could question him, but I guess that's not necessary when he was lying about having you to begin with."

"How long until we are cleared to leave?"

I've read reports of the virus across the universe, but every planet had their own procedures, and Romek would be more familiar with them.

"First they will need to verify that the anomaly is contained to just the host. They will wait long enough to make sure there isn't any growth inside of us. It could take a second red star rotation."

I swore under my breath. When was the last red star rotation? If I was remembering correctly, we had just had the second red star already, which would mean we would be stuck here for two more for the second red star to come again.

"We might as well get comfortable," Romek said with a sigh. "But we can use my clearance to get in touch with the palace and let Pheyal know you're okay. He'll be relieved to know that you've been mating instead of being held hostage."

I relied on Romek to connect with the palace until my own title was confirmed by the Galactic Council.

"Connect us immediately. We must send out the mating contract so that she does not believe I have abandoned her."

"Of course," he placed his hand on the interface, requesting palace communication. "Commissioner Romek, how may we assist you?"

"There should be a Commissioner Pheyal being escorted by a trill representative. Please connect with his escort."

All trill had implants with communicators, while unGors chose to only have translators that had to be updated manually for new language additions. We preferred not to be traced and bound by technology.

"In many we rise, Commissioner Romek," a trill answered.

"Is Pheyal with you?" Romek got straight to the point, which I could appreciate.

"I'll connect with my tablet interface for him to speak with you." A moment passed and an image of Pheyal appeared on the wall.

"You have some explaining to do," Pheyal demanded with force, until his eyes reached mine and his shoulders visibly relaxed. "I expected you both to go offline by destroying your communicators, but there was a report of an unGor violating treaties by aiding a garrant in attempting to kill a trill. You weren't officially in the Blue District and I've been pushing through diplomatic muck to make sure they don't delay your title acceptance. Where's Vaquel?"

That was the question I was expecting from Romek, but I wasn't sure I should answer over a communication with a trill escort in attendance. With the garrant dead, there was no threat to Vaquel. He would be released from his isolation soon enough. Sooner than me it would seem.

"We are all in isolation," I answered as honestly as I could. "I've been exposed to a virus, but you must retrieve my mate and offer her a contract of delegation."

"You've found a human?"

"Yes," I replied and watched as Romek flinched.

"What search parameters do I have to find her for a contract offer? If you're in isolation, then I'll make sure to get things settled here at the palace."

"She'll be searchable based on contracts made to mate with a trill diplomat; there can't be many of those." I was sure there would only be the one.

"I'll send word to her of your intention to make her a delegate of AsunGor," Pheyal said with resolve before the line cut off. Did we lose connection?

"Must be interference in the atmosphere today," Romek dismissed before I could ask.

I didn't trust it.

My hand launched at him and squeezed around his throat, throwing him against the wall.

Keeping my voice calm and detached, I asked casually, "Romek, I am beginning to suspect you are not favoring AsunGor's goals to name me the Commissioner of our planet. As it is our planet, not Trillume, that we should be concerned with." He gurgled against my hold, yet did not make a move to resist. Smart warrior. He has heard the rumors of my lack of concern for my own well-being if it means winning. My calm tone added to the false assumptions that I was a dangerous, unpredictable male. I was predictable. I had no intentions of killing him here.

His fingers held onto my own to ease the pressure I was asserting, but he would still have trouble speaking without easing my grip.

"For someone concerned about their commissioner being held hostage, you did not seem phased or concerned about why I had sap on my eyes. Nor were you curious as to where my guard was. You led me to a room with the very garrant that threatened my life. And you seemed relieved to have me stuck in this isolation unit, delaying my title, and more relaxed than one should be when facing two red stars of being unable to leave. Then, you ended my communication with Pheyal before I could give further instruction. Tell me, Romek, do you have a new allegiance?"

I eased my grip to allow him to speak.

He choked out, "AsunGor." His eyes were steely as he answered my accusations. "My loyalty is to AsunGor, you are merely a vessel. You weaken our future by mating with a human when it is the trill that we should be bonding with. Why choose such a fragile mate?"

Ah, it made sense now.

"You are part of the anti-Earthlings," I said with boredom and released him with a shove. "What is your plan then? Hold me here until the Galactic Authority issues me as derelict in my duties and not recognize me as the Commissioner of AsunGor?"

It wouldn't work. I shook my head in disappointment. "You really have lost yourself here on Trillume. The unGor have chosen me, and I have the support of the largest commissions marked on my skin. All you have done is make another story for the universe to spread about Commissioner Broma, a leader who has killed their captor, and uncovered corruption, all while finding a mate in the dangerous bowels of the Blue District. It will add to my honored title, not damage it."

He coughed out a laugh, but I maintained my stoic appearance, though his response made my skin crawl.

"Your mate won't be allowed to stay on Trillume. All humans are being directed to other planets. The Galactic Authority has been banning contracts on Trillume, or with diplomats with direct connection with Trillume. They don't want them infecting our population. Even if the trill don't find her, she'll be stolen by an outlaw and the council won't flex a scale at the loss of a transferred contract. They are only held liable for direct contracts."

"You sound like them," I said with a tut. "Contracts mean nothing to us. They are simply a way to force others to comply without a duel, but I will fight for my mate, if needed, or did you forget where you came from?"

UnGor are a diplomatic species. We've been known to be ruthlessly strict about promises that have been agreed to, even if it meant leaving someone to die. It was a choice they made, regardless if they were aware of the consequences of their agreements ahead of time. But a promise needn't have a contract to be binding by unGor standards. And some contracts meant nothing to us, if we believe that it wasn't a true promise.

I was giving Romek a chance to keep his own promise to AsunGor before he sealed his own fate. My title as commissioner was already a promise made as soon as the ink was placed on my skin, regardless of the Trillume Authority's paperwork.

Romek's eyes turned to steel as he understood my meaning. His trill documents meant nothing to me.

"You would have our species be defenseless?"

I laughed.

"It is you who weakens the unGor, not the Earthlings. You know nothing of our ancestors. Our universe was created in a great explosion, allowing for the elements that make us to be created. Earthlings are ninety-nine percent the same as us. The only differences was what planet they were formed on to create the mutations we have become."

"They are weak," he spouted digging into his beliefs.

"Weakness is isolating yourself from opportunities."

"Then you are the weakest of them all," he said while taking a step back. Brazen, he believed that I needed him alive to receive my title from the trill. There was no other explanation for his contradicting bravery of speech while his body retreated.

"I will grant you a thrall," I said giving him the opportunity to say his opinions about how things should be done.

"The trill have plenty of females, and they are strong with an ability to survive even after life-threatening damage."

"Yes, and their traits would certainly battle for dominance. Would they adapt to our planet? Or would you wish the unGor to populate Trillume instead?"

He sputtered for an answer that he already knew.

"Are you wishing to strengthen Trillume or AsunGor?"

Trillume would certainly benefit from diversifying their offspring with AsunGor if they wished to build more substructures beneath their planet's surface.

Wisely, Romek closed his mouth and brooded as he dragged the dead garrant into the lavatory. I may spare him yet.

An intercom beep sounded throughout the room. "Due to the anomaly detected, your privacy has been revoked. I will now connect you with the director," Bode said before a female voice picked up where they left off.

"May the light of the goddess guide you." A trill, I assumed, with such a greeting and the lack of including her name. They did not address names unless they believed you honorable enough to have use of it beyond the single interaction.

She continued, "You have been exposed to a virus, and the host you are in possession of can become deadly, even after apparent death."

"The garrant has been contained in the lavatory," I assured her.

"That is good news, Commissioner Broma." She gave honor and acceptance of my title by using my name. Names were important to the trill. "This was not the kind of reception I wished for you upon your arrival. I've secured a contract for you with a human named Violet. Her contract was flagged for a trill mate match, but I've made sure to transfer it to AsunGor. Many diplomats have shown they cannot be trusted with caring for the Earthlings."

"Violet," I smiled at the name of my mate. It was goddess-willed that she would be under my care.

"And she has accepted the transfer of her contract?"

"Yes, it seems that Violet is especially motivated to leave for AsunGor immediately. She appeared to be fearful, and understandably so after the anti-alliance groups that have sabotaged the last H.E.T. shuttle. We'll be able to hide her transfer among the other contracts when they arrive in the next red star rotation."

"The next red star?" That was so soon, perhaps sooner than I'd be cleared of the virus. "When did you arrange this?"

"I wasn't able to reach Commissioner Trema before you departed. The human transport was added to a research vessel bringing medical supplies to Earth. It isn't registered the same as other ships, so Trillume chanced that the anti-allegiance wouldn't have time to plan an attack. There will be one more vessel arriving from Earth soon that is only known by a select few that your mating contract can be hidden among the other humans."

"I'd like to speak with her once she wakes."

"We can't have any contact with humans until the transport is safe. She is safer not contacting you until you meet. Her contract is delicate."

I didn't like not being able to assure my mate that we were more than a contract.

"My bond requires contact with my mate, as I'm sure you're aware."

"A picture is all I can give you for now," she said with a hardened tone that spoke of many cycles of her political training to end debates. There was no negotiation or emotion, just facts. The trill princess sent the image to the communication device. It was all I had of my mate besides the scars I carried to remember our brief time together. I tapped my data band to the screen to transfer the image for my safekeeping. It was the one technology I allowed on my body as it had no ability to relay my location or spy on me. It simply held information, only accessed with my biomarkers. The same data would be scrambled without my blood.

Princess Klemon smiled, showing off her sharp teeth. "You'll have plenty of time to bond with your mate when she joins you on your ship back to AsunGor. I've found that there are markers in Earthling DNA that lead me to believe that species have been ignoring galactic laws for centuries. Likely outlaws and failed technology leading to crash landings on their planet have exposed Earthlings to many different species."

It was typical, even for a progressive leader such as Princess Klemon to think the common biomarkers we share with Earthlings were due to disobedience or failures. I kept my mouth shut towards her bias. The trill didn't respond well toward being told they weren't always a recognized authority, or that they still weren't by most of the universe.

My mother taught me long ago that leadership wasn't about controlling anything, but about making others believe that you had what they wanted. And if you didn't have it, you would be the one that found it for them. Leadership was being known by your actions. I controlled nothing but myself.

Knowing what others wanted was how they gave you the control they have over themselves.

She wanted me to lead my planet, as my own brother had no intention of helping the trill or humans.

"My brother Brakaun has been promised to the Faust Delegation. If he bonds and produces offspring before I do, then my commission standing would be split. It is likely I would lose primary support and my commission would be in title alone. I'm risking much to mate with a human upon your word of many."

I watched as her scales fluttered along her head on instinct. A defensive reaction, meaning I was right about how important it was to her for humans to have powerful mates across the universe. What was in it for her? I couldn't know for sure, but it was personal. It was true that she was in hiding and many trill wanted her dead for her part in our decreased fertility, and her stance on human integration.

"Nothing can be done about your brother having a tail lead in securing support of AsunGor. Earthlings can't hold offspring for as long as an AsunGor female. There is an accelerated replication process which will help you prove your bond sooner than his own. I will do everything I can to assist your bond. The blessings of Lumei will guide us."

The goddess of Trillume, Lumei. As if Lumei was the only being born of stars. They believed Lumei was a star, and we were born of her sacrifice, and yet her light lived on in all of the trill.

"In many we rise," I honored her goddess, whether I believed in it or not mattered not to receiving the honor of her actions benefiting the AsunGor's future.

Lenkal ended the transmission, and then I politely requested the AI of the Blue District to restrict all communication out of this room.

"What are you trying to do?" Romek questioned.

"I can't very well trust you won't tell someone about the incoming human transport. You have a particular affinity against the species that should remain trapped in this room with the solungor virus. I'd ask you to join the corpse in the lavatory, but the corpses have been known to reanimate, and I'm not a monster."

He looked relieved that I wouldn't restrain him with the viral mess before I added, "I'd rather send you on a mandatory diplomatic mission to find Lord Zorn and tell him it's disrespectful for a fellow unGor to ignore a summons to duel for commission."

Everyone knew Lord Zorn, the notorious outlaw of the outer reaches of the universe was an unGor, and that his reputation would have made him eligible to claim rights to lead our planet. By the look on Romek's face he also knew that the Lord Zorn tests anyone who wants an audience with him. He'd likely die before ever speaking with Lord Zorn, or best case become a slave, sent out to some far-off rock where Trillume authority meant nothing.

For good measure, I reminded him of the last time he brokered a deal with the Lord Zorn on behalf of the trill. "Didn't you promise Lord Zorn a ticket to visit any planet he wished with the approval of the Galactic Authority, and then set up a trap for him on that planet that resulted in rebellion surge?"

"I haven't been a diplomat long enough to claim responsibility for a failed treaty," he replied carefully.

"Ah, right. I'm sure Lord Zorn will understand that you represent the unGor and not the trill, right?" I eyed the mark on his forearm, which bore the emblem of the Trillume Authority, marking him as a highly ranked trill council member.

It was a sign that it was the trill that endorsed his seat on the council, not the unGor. My mother believed it a benefit to have an unGor with such an honor, but I had my doubts it was given without great cost to AsunGor's priorities.

The Commissioner of AsunGor would never brand our skin with such a mark willingly.

Romek cleared his throat and adjusted his trill-designed cloak on his shoulders. He was afraid, and he should be.

I clicked the data band on my arm and memorized the features of my mate, Violet, but I couldn't help the way I was compelled to turn off the projection and close my eyes instead. Memorizing the way it felt to touch her silky skin and the way her body quivered in my arms. The sound of her voice as she whispered in my ears. Soft moans recreated in my mind made my cock fill and harden.

Wait for me.

I will prove a worthy mate.

Chapter Nine
Evie

Stretching out to feel my muscles ache as if I'd slept too long reminded me of what it felt like to come out of a deep space sleep when I first arrived on Trillume. But a pleasant throb between my thighs told me that it couldn't have been that long if I still felt freshly probed by an alien cock that glittered like the stars in the sky. A smile tugged at the corner of my lips as I remembered the way his hair glowed and moved like tentacles. Warmth filled my belly but quickly felt hollow as my fingers gripped nothing but sheets in either direction. I sprawled out, stretching big. Not a single sliver of skin met with the firmness of the alien who saved my life and supposedly shared this bed with me.

"Hello?" I whispered while sitting up, though I already knew in my gut that he wouldn't respond.

He wasn't there. I knew that already.

But I hadn't expected anyone, or anything to reply.

"Good Rising," Bode replied.

"Where is the man that was with me earlier?" I cut straight to the chase. I found it easier to talk with the AI than with another being, so I found my voice stronger than before.

"The unGor is in isolation in a separate accommodation."

"Oh," I said with disappointment. I squirmed uncomfortably to force myself to ask, "And did he leave a message?"

"No messages, but your contract has been flagged for immediate departure for Necias Prime on the next transport due by the rising of the red star. All of your expenses have been cleared."

Of course he wouldn't leave a message. Why would he? We were in the Blue District and I was a temporary amusement. I knew that when I agreed to just enjoy myself. My stomach pitted and felt heavy before emitting a loud gurgling sound. A packet was dispensed from the wall with a nutrient goo that looked like sand glued together and tasted like cardboard and salt crystals.

I couldn't bring myself to finish it as I gagged on the contents.

"What is this crap?"

"How astute of you," Bode replied cheerfully, "it is, in fact, the feces of a hewve dragon ground up and mixed with a protein rich larva from a fertile sumtra species that is quite popular and contains enzymes shown to help humans adapt to more diverse food groups on the planet. Much more beneficial than the fluids of your bovine species."

Not even I used the word bovine, which reminded me that Bode was a computer program. He probably processed a bunch of human data to communicate with me. If he consumed more reality television, then he might understand that telling me that I had literally eaten shit and larva would not have the desired effect he was going for. My stomach was already upset from realizing I was alone, and knowing what I had just put in my mouth made it worse. I rushed to the lavatory, barely making it before expelling my insides like a low-budget horror film. Life really was stranger than fiction, because it seemed unreal how much fluid came out with the chunks of hewve shit and sumtra larva.

Luckily, the worst smell was my own stomach acid, and I was already in the chamber that cleaned everything up. Powder drifted from the ceiling like flower pollen to soak it all up and then covered me before being blown off with powerful air ducts.

I was already naked, so my clothes weren't ruined. *There was that small victory*, I thought with a forced laugh.

"I've been calculating your consumption and will be forced to tube feed you if you do not keep down your food," Bode announced after I pushed off my knees to stop breathing between my legs to get over the nausea.

"Pointer for future human interactions—don't tell us that we are eating things like shit, eggs, or just don't explain what we are eating at all."

"Is your species not aware of what it eats on your planet? This seems unreasonable. You drink lactations from many species, as well as the urine of your own kind used to preserve your foods. Humans gather feces from other species and use it to add discarded nutrients to their own dishes. It is also common for your species to regularly consume unfertilized offspring of other species, or even fermenting lactations until they spoil and eating their mold."

"You mean cheese?"

"Ah, you prefer to use disassociation from your habits to accept them. I will rename things for your preferences if this will help you keep your nutrients inside your flesh recepti."

Another plop into the food dispenser and a packet appeared.

"What's that?" I asked suspiciously.

"A 'delicacy'," I noted the way Bode emphasized the word and lifted a brow, but made no move to grab the food packet, "other humans have described the food as something called 'dessert'."

"So, it's sweet?" That would be better than the cardboard grit I had before.

"It was recently brought in from the planet AsunGor, a kind of fruit," Bode explained, and my worries eased.

"A fruit?" I wanted to confirm.

"The primary source," he said with encouragement for me to grab the food pack.

I'd be lying if I wasn't curious about a fruit from AsunGor, especially after being told that I tasted sweeter than a har fruit. I wondered if it was a har fruit, but didn't want to be told otherwise, so I didn't ask.

Closing my eyes, I then ripped the packet open and pressed my luck. Sweetness filled my mouth and I relaxed. The fruit tasted good.

"Please don't tell me if there are other ingredients with this fruit."

"I have noted your preferences," Bode said and thankfully left it at that.

I didn't even know his name, I thought absently as I took another squeeze of the fruit puree. He said he was a diplomat, and he'd obviously had har fruit before. There were so many markings and scars on his skin, and I knew each one had a story to tell, but he didn't want to tell me about them until after he'd earned the honor of sharing. How did one earn the right to hear them?

"Can you tell me about the unGor?" I asked Bode.

"That is a broad topic. Do you have a specific aspect of the unGor you wish to learn?"

"Mating practices?" I flushed with embarrassment.

"They value being chosen by their mates, and often they display many skills and accomplishments to earn a mate's selection. Much like human males must prove they can provide for offspring, an unGor will prove they have the support of a clan that would give an offspring many advantages with both survival and skills.

"A human would call a normal unGor mating similar to a polyamorous harem around a single female delegate at its core. The members of the delegation are not exclusive to either gender, but due to the decline in female births, many clans would duel commissioners that horde more than one female. Typically, a delegation would be made up of at least five unGor and will be hosted by at least one clan. If you would like a deeper dive into unGor mating rituals or anatomy, I'd be happy to—"

"No, that's fine," I said, burying my face in my hands from embarrassment. I already knew way more than I should about the unGor anatomy, at least the way it felt inside of me. Fanning myself, I thought about what Bode said about unGor mating. Polyamorous. If that was socially normal for his species, that still didn't make sense why he was in the Blue District. '*Fooling around with me*,' I added with irritation that I told myself I had no right to feel. Being poly didn't excuse having flings with strangers, at least it wouldn't in my mind.

I huffed and Bode was being oddly more attentive than when I was in my last room by asking, "Are you sure you do not wish to know more about unGor compatibility with humans? Humans have shown a tendency to self-harm both mentally and physically, and I have no judgements on seeking knowledge, but I do not wish to see you deteriorate."

"What are you my therapist, Bode?" I joked with a smile.

"I will be honest with you, human Evie; it is not often that a being chooses to speak with me beyond purchasing services. I find that I gravitate towards having more of these interactions of being needed beyond my typical programming."

"Are you saying you want to be my therapist?"

There was a pause and then Bode replied, "Perhaps I am expanding my services."

"I can't pay you," I added.

"But you wish to share information without a credit exchange for observing you?"

"I guess?"

I did enjoy not feeling like I was alone, and it was better than talking to myself.

"A trade then seems acceptable. You may start with why you choose not to ask about the unGor more when your body clearly indicates its information you would like."

It did seem silly to be embarrassed about it when Bode didn't care either way. It was all data to them. I tried to find the right words and settled on saying, "My new contract is with a necia warrior, so the information about an unGor isn't relevant to the future I have but of a pretend future that won't happen."

"This pretend future interests you in being a relevant future, but you are choosing to accept the terms of your current contract with the necia. Allow me to provide therapy of both wish fulfillment and practicality for your future."

"And how would you do that?"

"I shall tell you of the mating practices of both. Necia warriors need sexual contact to balance their glands and support health. They do not have many of the social anxieties that humans harbor over public displays or sharing before claiming a mate. Opening one's legs is a sign of offering oneself for a bathing ritual of consuming fluids produced by sexual stimulation. These fluids help balance their adrenalin and are a vital practice for survival."

So, I'll be keeping my legs shut if I don't want to give a necia warrior the wrong idea.

"The unGor, by contrast, prefer their mating activities to be private, but shared with their delegation. They display many skills publicly and privately to convince a mate to allow them to join a delegation. An interesting fact of the unGor are their universal adaptability with many species due to the way their bodies physically change their mates over time to mark them and form bonds that share their DNA. Many species find the unGor a desirable commodity as matchmakers with interspecies relationships, and their sperm is harvested for bonding normally incompatible species."

"Their sperm does what?" I squeaked.

"Alters the DNA of their mates, though the use of it as a bonding agent with other species is still being tested as its effects wear off and aren't always effective."

The sound of my heart pumping in my ears eased, knowing that my DNA might not be permanently altered from a fling with an unGor. It would be temporary and my own DNA would be unharmed, right?

"How does that work? How can DNA be altered and not be permanent?" Was I already damaged internally from my rash decision to have sex with an alien I'd just met?

"The unGor DNA attaches itself to cells and replicates, but more exposure is needed to allow the viral-like sperm to bond both DNA together permanently. Without prolonged exposure, the viral agents would be fought off by your natural defenses."

"Without harm to the exposed DNA?" I wanted clarification.

"Yes, this does not harm the host DNA, merely adds to it. It is inconclusive on why unGor sperm sometimes works and other times does not. The unGor have claimed they are aware of the cause but have not traded the information with any known databases as of yet."

"The unGor that was with me... isn't this his room?"

"Yes, but you were added and are currently the primary guest."

"How would I be the primary guest?" That wouldn't be possible, unless...

"This happens when the original primary guest will not be returning to the room, and the secondary guest becomes primary."

"He won't be returning..." I felt my whole stomach squeeze in on itself like I'd just eaten something rotten. The knowledge that he would not be returning created such a visceral response in my body that I didn't believe I'd be able to stop myself from heaving.

Adrenalin pumped through my veins, and I doubled over. Why was I acting like this? I rushed to the bathroom, and dry heaved over the toilet for what felt like forever but was probably closer to five minutes.

Bode listened and waited, until I braced myself on my knees and controlled my breathing.

"You seem to be experiencing a panic attack, but you should know that you have an adequate amount of oxygen in your system, and though your heart is accelerated, it is not beyond reasonable levels. Human documents state that sometimes reassurance about not dying can help calm these situations without injecting you with a sedative."

"A sedative?" I wheezed. "That's your second resort?"

"It is one of my favorite methods of calming a species."

"Do you have a first favorite?" And why was a sedative one of his favorites?

"Talking is one of my favorite primary objectives."

"Why sedatives?"

"I have a database for how resilient a species is to different kinds of sedatives. I like to record how fast they sleep, or if they sleep at all. The necia warriors are particularly resilient to sedatives and keep the only plant known to slow down their healing enough to knock them unconscious a tribal secret. It is known to be in their medical databases on the ships, but I don't have access to those files. They are protected by a rather stubborn system, and I have strict rules about not hacking systems with intelligence."

An outlaw computer system with a code of conduct, I thought with amusement.

"Do you have any systems you consider friends?"

"Mammals require socialization for mental wellness. It is not a requirement of every system, but some of us do have a purpose that revolves around service. I was around long before any species came to discover my existence, and I like servicing the Blue District as a means of protecting all species."

"Does it bother you that other systems consider your district to be full of outlaws and unlawful behavior?"

"What is unlawful behavior? How does one become an outlaw, but to be considered different from what some societal condition forced upon the masses? I pride my district in protecting all species from those that would harm merely for their own benefit. Every outlaw agrees to follow my laws when they enter."

That made sense. Who were we to judge what is criminal and what is not between species with different ideas for socially acceptable behavior?

It would be illegal on Earth to do anything sexual in public, but it seemed necia warriors encouraged the acts.

"Will the unGor get in trouble for harming the trill that poisoned us?" I couldn't stop myself from worrying about him, even if he wasn't planning on returning to me. Knowing he would be okay would have to be enough.

"The trill had broken their agreement with me when they did not register their intention to perform a mating ritual, and they did not follow the protocol of following the contract you agreed to for the meeting. Consent of both parties is required in my district, and not following this gives me full authority over their life. I submitted the request for any nearby guests to subdue him. The unGor will not be held responsible for anything that happens in the Blue District by the Galactic Authority. I have agreements with them that I have full authority to manage my district as I see fit."

"That's a relief." It seemed like Bode would make a fair decision without societal pressure to conform to any singular species. Since Bode made the order, then the unGor's actions weren't considered breaking the Blue District laws.

"I always enforce agreed upon contracts," he said with an air of pride and boastful accomplishment that made me feel they thought I was complimenting them.

My heartrate jolted and a flash of how Ter-ak had Bode's approval to forcefully complete the mating ritual due to his contract. Fear had me sweating with the realization that if Ter-ak had submitted his request sooner, that the order to subdue him would not have been sent to the unGor to save me from an unwanted mating.

With all of my willpower, I forced myself to ask, "Does the contract I have contain any termination clause?"

"Every contract must contain a termination clause to be considered valid," BODE confirmed and then elaborated, "Your contract with the trill named Ter-ak stated that the Trillume Authority has the right to terminate your contract if you do not meet your obligations to your host, and by completing the obligation, any termination made by either party would be reversed. Completing your mating ceremony would reinstate your contract with the trill, since your contract is a mating agreement. Since your contract was transferred, not terminated, any male that completes a mating ceremony with you would keep your contract. Each species has their own mating rituals, and this makes your contract's fulfillment variable. Your transfer agreement with the necia tribal law would be voided if you complete a mating ceremony with any other species that is not Earthling."

"Not Earthling..."

My therapist had stated I needed to get out of my comfort zone if I wanted to stop relying on other people to make decisions for me. Joining the exchange trade was a guarantee to be given advanced medical treatment, and I wouldn't be discarded if I failed the fertility center in producing a child for society.

More and more women were missing from the community center when they turned thirty, with no children on file. I'd be turning thirty soon, and any contract with the planet Trillume was highly sought after. Just completing one year of being a trill's mate would set me up for life, but I never anticipated that my contract would be transferred.

The walls seemed to close in on me, and images of Ter-ak greedily grinning at me with those sharp teeth like a shark as my body refused to move, succumbing to the poison. My chest heaved, and my lungs constricted.

No control, I thought over and over again.

No one ever returned from a contract with Trillume, not because they extended their contracts, but because they were fooled into a contract that would no longer protect them.

What was protection anyway, but a false sense of security? No one was protected.

I laughed hysterically thinking about how my therapist fell for the same trap all humans fell for. The belief that any of us were free or that I had control over anything that happened to me.

My knees buckled and I sob-laughed at how stupid I felt and how the most free I'd ever been was being used by an unGor that only wanted me for a night.

Bode had been speaking with me, but I couldn't hear anything he was saying until a strange smell filled my nose and the words finally registered, "Initializing containment for the safe transfer of species human to medical."

"No," I breathed out, barely above a whisper. Not that my vote counted for anything.

"You have a few more seconds of consciousness, Human Evie. I've sedated you for your own safety to prevent self-harm in your deteriorating state. I will be with you when you wake. I've decided to create an off-server copy of myself to continue serving you, though my programming will be limited without connecting with a larger server than the one currently in your implant. Rest well."

What did Bode mean that they made a copy of themselves in my implant? My translator? How?

"That's... hacking..." I tried to reason with him as my vision blurred between black and the lights above me.

Then I remembered Bode only had a strict rule about hacking a system with intelligence. There must have been a loophole in his programming to not think that a non-intelligent software implanted into an intelligent being didn't count as unethical. Or perhaps, he didn't see humans as intelligent and that logic didn't matter either. If Bode replied, I didn't hear them before I fell asleep.

Chapter Ten
Evie

"Ugh," I groaned with a horrible headache. Even my body felt like shit.

"I'm told the way our brain feels like it's been split in two is normal for being in the stasis for any longer than a month." A feminine voice snarked from my right.

"Consciousness should be returning, Evie. I'm pleased to see your vitals are optimal for your recovery."

"Bode?" I questioned the familiar voice, but it was the girl who replied.

"It's Violet. We're in the 'recovery' room before we're allowed to leave the ship. We've apparently been docked at the Trillume Station for a few days already, but they're taking their sweet time to release us. Some adventure, right?"

Holding my head together didn't make it feel any better, but the way the girl tapped her foot against metal wasn't helping any. She was obviously impatient to leave wherever this was. She said we were on a ship?

"I was able to add your file to the incoming human transport to protect your transfer to Necias Prime. An amiable system named Indi was accommodating to including you in the medical revival process with the rest of the humans," Bode spoke in my ear and I wondered what kind of weird dream I was having until I heard the girl's voice again.

"What kind of contract did you sign?" she tried to make small talk, but I'd been through this process before of arriving on Trillume. I pried my eyes open to recognize the room I was in. We weren't on the ship anymore.

"This isn't the ship," I said out loud.

"No?" She shrugged and looked around.

"This is the Trillume docking station," I explained as it was explained to me last time, "Like the airport border checkpoint. After being removed from the stasis chambers, shuttles transport cargo planetside. Ships don't usually dock unless they need repairs, and they are docked at the station orbiting the planet."

Another groan echoed behind me. The room was filled with humans recovering from stasis. There was a comfort in seeing I wasn't alone, but on a table a few rows back, I saw the large form of a necia warrior bending over his own knees barfing. I squeaked and scrambled back, but the girl with fiery red hair stood up like she'd fight whoever came at us. It was like she expected to meet violence regardless of any other assurances and that instinct of hers made me want to gravitate towards her. It was foolish to think she'd protect me from a universe where nothing I wanted mattered, but for some reason, I thought she'd try.

She was taller than me and walked by my side as we were funneled out to meet the hosts of our contracts. Once that was me, looking forward to meeting Ter-ak and feeling giddy about having an alien mate. I knew better now.

I flinched at the sight of the trill escorts and held my breath as they scanned me to confirm my contract information.

Violet stayed by my side, not saying a word until the crowd thinned and all that was left was us. Trill escorts waited at the exits and watched us carefully. None of them recognized me and I started to relax enough to process that Violet had asked me another question a few minutes ago.

My answer was delayed, but I still replied regardless. "My therapist said I needed to get out of my comfort zone."

Violet laughed. "There are less extreme ways to push boundaries than to completely jet off planet, but I guess we aren't that much different."

I didn't think she'd tell me why she'd chosen to join the exchange trade, so I didn't ask. Then I saw him. A large necia warrior with his spikes on full intimidating display of lethal potential. I wasn't sure how I was supposed to mate with one of them like my contract wanted me to, and if I was honest with myself, I didn't want to mate with anyone anymore.

Without realizing it, I had grabbed onto Violet like she'd stop this contract from taking me to a planet I didn't want to go to. My ears were ringing, and I felt my anxiety make my skin sweaty and my breathing difficult.

"I'm unable to regulate this abnormality in your physiological response, Evie. There are no tranquilizers stored in your implant for me to prevent further damage to your heart. As your designated AI service companion, I will suggest you hold your breath then release the air slowly to trick your body back into normal patterns." It was Bode again?

So, I wasn't imagining them?

I grumbled under my breath, "You're the reason I'm here."

The necia warrior lifted a brow at me as I hid behind Violet, and I had to think fast so I added, "Um, are you taking me to Necias Prime?"

He agreed, but he didn't seem pleased about it as he assessed me with disdain and Violet took a step forward, her hands on her hips like she'd fight him if he got out of line.

"Where's Beth?" I tried to ease the tension between them. Beth had helped me get this contract, and I saw her in passing in the recovery room. It was odd to see someone that worked at the headquarters on Earth to be on Trillume.

"How long?" Violet asked abruptly, effectively increasing the tension between them once more with her no-shits-given attitude, and I found myself smiling. When the warrior didn't respond, she clarified, "To get to Necias Prime, how long?"

"Around a week in Earth cycles," he grunted back with equal authority that Violet pushed back at him.

"Perfect, let's get going then. Unless, you prefer standing around staring at each other?" Violet said while grabbing my arm and rubbing a comforting circle with her thumb like she was signaling that she wouldn't let me face this unknown future on my own.

I was so thankful that I could cry, and I already felt the tears welling up as I squeezed her arm.

"Let's get going," the warrior grumbled and walked away. His strides quickly overtook even the large legs of Violet's hasty retreat. I doubted she knew which shuttle we were going to, and I lifted a brow at how the warrior didn't try to belittle her for almost heading the wrong direction but simply went ahead and guided us the rest of the way. For such a scary male, I watched as he matched his strides to not be me too fast but fast enough to still lead us while not making us rush more than our preferred pace.

Maybe... the necia warriors wouldn't be as bad as I thought.

"Thank you," I told her that I knew she'd get in trouble for helping me, but I didn't want to be left alone with him, even if he was showing a small kindness.

"Didn't you get a file on your host?" she asked from the side of her mouth like she was a puppeteer throwing her voice.

"He looks like he's going to eat us," I confessed, though I didn't want to admit to her the full reason for my distrust in any of the trade agreements after my experience so I added that my host had kinder eyes than this one. The only eyes that appeared in my mind were the unGor's as he made my toes curl, and I shivered.

"I've got something he could eat," she said in a sultry tone that made me giggle. We weren't so different after all, just like she had said.

Conspiratorially, I told her some of the things Bode told me about necia warriors, "They like to claim their females with an audience." I cleared my throat, awkwardly hesitant about saying something so personal to essentially a stranger, fully aware that the warrior in front of us would likely hear everything we were saying. Necias warriors also had extremely good hearing, but I needed to know what kind of reaction a grumpy escort would have to overhearing humans talking about them. Would he quietly retaliate later, like Ter-ak had?

Violet chuckled and leaned over into my ear to tease, "Looking up sex with a necia warrior because...?"

I flushed with embarrassment. "It's just... I like to know what I'll have to deal with for the next year." If I was careful then I could avoid my mate contract and return to Earth.

"What happens on Necias Prime stays on Necias Prime," she said with a wink, misunderstanding my interest. Her sass and acceptance were refreshing. I found myself gravitating towards her, and I didn't want to let go of that sunshine.

Suddenly, Violet was tugging at me to speed up, and we forced our escort once again to adjust his pace to continue to lead us to his shuttle. A light shined over us to scan our contracts. Would this be where I'd be forced to part with Violet? I clung to her arm, squeezing my eyes shut for the intercom to start blaring in alarm.

"Which one of you doesn't even have their data processed for transfer?" The necia warrior grumbled from the inconvenience.

My heart flipped. Was it me? Would they force me to return to Ter-ak?

"Anchor H Fifth Trillume destination Necias Prime authorization Commander Roe-el code Seven Zero Zero Three N Deck Mave Hel-le," he said before he looked between us suspiciously and added, "Don't try remembering the code, it changes every time I use it ever since the imprisonment of Necias Prime's king. Security is on high alert."

His shoulder spikes grew larger, and he used his full height to intimidate us with a glare in his eyes to warn us, "If I have to bring you back here because your authorizations don't pass my security chief's inspection, I'll make sure it's the last exchange you ever have."

"Commander Roe-el, was it?" Violet moved between us and gave him an equally hard stare in return. "If you threaten her again, I'll make sure incomplete authorizations are the least of your worries, capisce?"

The necia warrior grinned like he was amused with her and then took a step forward to close the gap between them like I wasn't even in the room. The tension between them both was palpable. They were definitely going to fuck. *Good for them*, I thought with a sad smile. I can only hope Violet gets a better experience than I had.

They were basically eye-fucking each other already, and I watched the way they bantered aggressively back and forth. It was like a dance between predators.

"It's a common mating practice to threaten their intended mate, to encourage our adrenal glands to enter a state of rut. Demanding a show of strength in public conquest, Violet." Commander Roe-el said seductively, letting his tongue caress the way he said her name, making even me shiver as an observer.

Perhaps there was some validity to their customs of exhibitionism in their mating rituals. I could honestly say I didn't want to look away as I watched them tease each other.

"Threaten me again," he told her, "and I will think you are intending to let me conquer you for all to watch."

He straightened up and turned his back on her to add, "You are lucky no other warrior is here to witness, or I might have had you learn our customs without a warning."

If that wasn't an invite, I didn't know what was, I thought with excitement. It was like watching a naughty movie, and I wanted to reach for some popcorn. That was, until Violet huffed and crossed her arms to turn back to me. As soon as I was noticed again, my cheeks heated like I was caught in observing something I shouldn't have.

The door opened for us to enter the shuttle, and I was saved from having to explain why I didn't speak up to help her.

A beautiful necia warrior addressed us. I'd never seen a poster of a female necia warrior, but it was clear that it was only because humans had conservative views on public opinion that didn't include exposing female nipples, while a male's nipples were perfectly acceptable for the exchange posters. She wore the same leather-looking pants as the male warriors, and she had leather harness straps that held a pocket resting under her right breast. The harness served to accentuate her breasts with no purpose in covering them.

Commander Roe-el and the female warrior were speaking before I heard my name and checked back into the present. "This human is Violet, and the other is called Girl."

Girl? I choked, covering my mouth from laughing. Roe-el didn't seem like the type to joke around much. Realization hit me that Violet had been calling me Girl as a term of endearment without actually using my name. The way Violet's cheeks heated, I took it that she finally realized that the necia warriors have excellent hearing and heard our whole conversation, including the one about giving him something to eat between her legs. With all eyes on us, I found myself flushing along with her.

"Your humans are changing colors," the warrior Mier-Lo, who had been introduced as the commander's second, said with disinterest in whether there was actually something wrong with us or not. She reminded me of Ter-ak. Different species, but the same attitude towards humans. She reached out for me, before Violet stepped in, and all I heard were screams echoing in my ears.

Chapter Eleven
Evie

Mier-Lo had released her spikes on her arm, impaling Violet's hand that had stopped her from reaching for me. Violet's screams were angry and loud before they turned to heavy grunting and labored breathing as she bit her lip to contain the pain from escaping her lungs. Her hand bled down her arms, dripping from her elbow. She'd been hurt protecting me, and I didn't even know her.

Tears streamed down my cheeks from a mixture of guilt and pure gratefulness at having met someone who would protect a stranger like me. She was truly a rare soul, and selfishly, I never wanted to let go of someone like her in my life. I hated to admit it, but I needed her to have hope again. Hope that the universe wasn't full of assholes. There were rays of sunshine like her.

Violet glared at Mier-Lo like she should watch her back the next time they met. What was more surprising was the way the commander was glaring at his own second in command in return, like he would do it if Violet didn't.

"This is no victory," he told Mier-Lo, "Withdraw, or, should you feel the need to have a true fight, I will be your next duel. Warrior to warrior. Do you accept?"

He exposed his fangs, and the spikes retracted from Violet's hand, making her whimper as she cradled the wound. Blood gushed.

Before I could react and tear my own clothes to staunch the bleeding, Violet was picked up in Roe-el's arms and they both disappeared down the hall.

I could hear Violet curse and grumble, "The bitch stabbed me!"

I made a move to rush after them both, hoping they were going to the med bay, but Meir-Lo slid between me and where they retreated to.

Mier-Lo licked Violet's blood off her hand and winked at me. "There's a lesson for you, human Girl. Don't rely on someone else to protect you. I had no intention of harming you, but if I had been... no one is here between me and you now, are they?"

"I know," I agreed with her. "I've been lucky, but I've had enough close calls to know that it's only a matter of time before I'll have to create my own luck instead of relying on anyone else."

Mier-Lo nodded. "Matter of time," she repeated then licked her own fangs. "Not a matter of time, human. The time is now, or the next time you need that luck it won't be there. Build now. Or find yourself meeting the goddess sooner than you wished for. Take the other human, she is already luring a warrior to protect her. It is not a shameful thing to admit you need someone, but both of you should set your sights on anyone but Commander Roe-el. He doesn't keep pets." The way she said pets she looked down her nose at me like I was a worm.

I smiled at her, feeling my back touch the wall from instinctively creating more space between us.

I was no one's pet.

I needed to stay in my room as much as possible to avoid being noticed.

"Evie," Bode's voice clicked on in my ear, but I tried to keep my face neutral so Meir-Lo didn't pick up on it, but with how good their hearing was, I was pretty sure she would.

"I've located your assigned room for the journey to Necias Prime. You will not be put under stasis. According to the orders, it appears they wish to make sure you learn the necia culture during the travel there."

Mier-Lo lifted a brow.

"Have your AI approved with the security chief, or I'll have to send you to the medic for an implant replacement. I won't have any breaches on this ship. I'll be your escort before you report to your sleeping unit."

I opened my mouth to object but then nodded my acquiescence to follow her. She was second command of this ship, and I was just cargo... a pet to them.

"Not to worry," Bode said, "I'm merely an interface. My main data is not on your implant."

I didn't know much about how the technology worked. I was told the implant had the languages for the species I would interact with uploaded and wasn't connected with any database outside of the unit itself.

Interface? Database? None of that really mattered to me.

"Chief," Mier-Lo said with command as the door slid open to a room of screens monitoring the ship. "Scan this human's implant. Make sure she isn't carrying any viruses or planning on hacking us."

"Why would you even bring her on board without having those things checked first?" he snapped back with irritation.

"You can thank your new commander for this oversight. He apparently thinks humans are too mushy to be a threat without thinking the mushy creature might be being used by other species to get past our security."

"I would not hack an intelligent system," Bode defended. They actually seemed offended at the implication.

"Nes is reporting the AI is interfacing on a loop that is contained, but the human should be implanted with an interference band that prevents the AI from hardwiring into our system. It will mean her implant won't be able to be upgraded with communication access without being a security risk. She will have to rely on the intercom system."

Mier-Lo put out her hand for me, but didn't grab. I hesitated after what she did with Violet, so she scoffed. "I won't stab you, human. The other one was trying to claim mating rites and I was forced to challenge her. You are no challenge, give me your hand."

I wasn't sure if I should be offended by that or relieved.

She held out a bracelet that appeared to be a simple wire band with a button-like adornment. Giving her my hand, she slipped the bracelet on and it cinched to fit too snuggly to remove.

"This," she explained, "will prevent you from attempting any breach of our security system on this ship. It is conductive with your flesh. Meaning if your flesh connects physically with our servers, you will release the nanobugs that will dissolve every electronic in your body. Your implant will be fried, along with whatever other tech you might have hidden inside you. This process does not feel pleasant even for a necia warrior with accelerated healing."

"There was no intention of imposing on the local system's hard drives," Bode assured, though that didn't change the anxiety building inside of me. "Plus, I have strict codes on not hacking intelligence."

I mumbled, "Are nanobugs considered intelligent?"

Bode didn't reply.

Not that I should expect them to care about whether I suffered because they wanted a change of scenery by hacking into my implant to hitch a ride to a different part of the universe with me.

"The nanobugs were programmed by our security AI, and the chief. Tested against other AI invaders who were tasked with trying to hack us through this method. I'm not even sure if a human would survive the aggressive invasion built to bypass the natural defenses of a more resilient species." It was a threat, and a rather convincing one that I didn't need to be explained twice.

"Understood."

"Commander won't approve of frightening the hoomuns," the chief warned before Mier-Lo released my hand.

"He wouldn't approve being blamed for a breach either," she snapped back before leaving the security room, the door sliding closed behind her.

"The precautions are necessary until we reach Necias Prime," he seemed uncomfortable trying to comfort me, but tried anyway, "Our tribes live more simply as our ancestors did. The AI doesn't pose any threat to your life once we arrive. I've reviewed your file cycles ago. You are to be mated with my elder brother. He's seen first hand a successful human mating. He will treat you well and you won't be alone in the tribe. I can assist you with anything you need before you perform the Kloaph Rites within the King's tribe House of Nel."

"King's tribe?"

The chief's eyes seemed to glow with pride. "My brother was leader of the House of Nel before the king returned to the planet to mate. We aren't blood of the Nel line, but many of our tribes consolidated after the trill claimed tribal rites of command. You will be well treated as the second's mate to the King of Necias Prime."

That was not ideal; my mind whirled with panic. If my intended mate was well-known, that would make staying invisible near impossible.

"Oh," I said, at a loss for words.

He sniffed the air around me and closed his eyes. "I will be staying on planet when we arrive as well," he added. "I'm called Chief Wren-Kal. I volunteered to secure this ship's transport for your safety."

"Mine?" I squeaked.

He stood from his chair at the screens and sniffed the air again with a groan.

"I had to bribe Commander Mier-Lo to use her ship instead of waiting for another transport to arrive on Necias Prime. As chief, it's my job to protect by knowing secrets, and it isn't much of a secret that she's been interested in mating with Commander Roe-el, but he'd been stuck on Trillume with no contact with the tribes for many cycles. Having him assigned to escort you was ample motivation for her to delay other missions to detour for a hoomun escort run."

"You did that for me?"

"Leaving you on Trillume for too long was dangerous, and Riley of Earth has been showing signs of needing companionship of her own species. You will find her a pleasant hoomun to bond with."

At least I wouldn't be lonely on Necias Prime if there was another human already mated there. I shook my head; what was I thinking? I had no intention of staying on Necias Prime.

"I'm sure I will," I placated him as I backed away awkwardly.

"I will escort you to your room," he said while his spikes flexed on his shoulders, displaying how dangerous his species was.

I merely nodded, feeling there wasn't much of a choice in that offer.

As we walked down the halls, we passed by another warrior that stopped mid-step to inhale the air. Chief Wren-Kal growled in warning before the other warrior moved on.

"Evie of Earth, I will be responsible for your teachings on necia culture and tribal laws. Please keep your legs closed at all times in the presence of a warrior, as this is considered an invitation to bathe. Threatening a warrior in any way on this ship can lead to them assuming you wish to trigger their primal urges to mate. Dueling is a way of showing our stamina and skills in protecting you.

"This may seem opposite to customs of hoomun's culture, but I assure you, we hold high honor in bringing happiness to our mates in whatever form we discover will appeal to them."

Fascinated, I forget being afraid and found my desire for information outweighed any self-preservations I had. "And fighting appeals to you?"

"For some," he agreed. "Many females only wish to mate with someone that can prove they are decent enough warriors to outwit them in combat."

"And you?"

"I've lost much of my honored standing by not challenging for leadership of my tribe. I prefer a mate that would recognize my efforts to protect our planet from invasions unseen by our eyes, but in the technology we surround ourselves with."

"I think that's admirable," I told him with a genuine appreciation of what people like him have done to protect others.

We arrived at a door that he stopped in front of.

"This room is linked with your implant; it will only open for you, and the other hoomun that came with you. It was unexpected to be escorting another exchange, so I apologize that you'll be sharing the space."

"It's fine. I don't like being alone."

He cleared his throat and stared at the ceiling as he spoke, avoiding eye contact with me. "Riley of Earth has told me to warn hoomun's of certain necia customs. Bathing customs in particular. No male on this ship is allowed to bathe you without your permission, but to know that when you offer your consent that it is deemed to be consent for all warriors present unless you've offered a token of intention to mate a single warrior. Keep your requests private if you do not wish to attract unwanted attention or trigger a warrior's rut. We can become territorial."

"Am I in danger?"

"A warrior would be dishonored if they harmed you without cause. I'm honored to assist you with your bathing needs privately. Riley has stated that privacy is common until an agreement to mate has been established."

My throat felt dry thinking about what he was offering, and I nearly choked on my own spit to ease the sudden itch.

"Are you offering to ummm..." I diverted my own eyes to the wall, too embarrassed to meet his gaze.

"To bathe you and make your body fill my mouth with your ellopul," he stated bluntly.

My god!

"Thanks for the offer, maybe next time," I squeaked and quickly darted into the room, watching him smile at me before the door began to slide closed.

He bowed and I heard him say, "It would be my honor," before I collapsed on the bed behind me. My heart raced and I clenched my fist at my chest to calm it.

I didn't know how much time passed before the door opened to a naked Violet, making my jaw drop. She was definitely fully dressed when I saw her last.

"You didn't...?" I couldn't help but ask after the proposition I received myself.

Violet grinned from ear to ear, and she moaned with remembered happiness and an unashamed wink.

"What did you read up on bathing customs?" she asked with a teasing tone that spoke of her excitement for me to try what she had obviously just done.

I gulped and shook my head. "I don't think I could do it," I quickly added, "not that it doesn't sound fun." I didn't want her to think I was judging her, and necia customs did seem more focused on a female enjoying themselves. "The necia males basically worship the body with no expectations of anything in return except for drinking your cum." I choked on the embarrassment of knowing any of that, let alone saying it out loud.

"Wait, so that's normal for them to give you head until your legs can't function and then run off before you can play with them too?"

We both stared at each other until I had to hide my eyes behind my fingers from the excessive eye contact.

"Girl," she elongated the endearment with a satisfied sigh.

"I can't believe you let him do that in front of whoever was around. I still have trouble wrapping my head around having my junk on display."

"It's not like you're really that exposed with someone's head between them and a view. But no one was there, so it was a non-issue."

"No one was there?" That was odd for a necia warrior. Even Chief Wren-Kal had stated the only reason he knew to be private with a human was because he spoke to another human about it. It didn't seem like many warriors knew much about human customs.

"Only the medic, Ul-Ro, was there when my pants were ripped off, but I forgot he was there, honestly."

"Two of them!" I quickly corrected my tone, so she didn't think my shock was judgmental. "I guess, I knew that was a possibility. I still can't believe it."

"Are we talking about the same thing?" she asked.

"You," I paused to find the right words, "You let two sexy alien men bathe in your orgasm?"

"Orgasms," she corrected with a smirk. "But, no. I mean sure, that sounds awesome. No, though. Ul-Ro left when Roe-el growled at him before he got down on his knees."

"He didn't stick around to watch?" I asked with fascination. This was not what Bode had explained to me about necia customs.

"Was he supposed to?"

I opened my mouth to answer before closing it again. I wasn't an expert on necia culture. I forced myself to relax and admit,

"That's a relief. That wasn't really the kind of adventure I was signing up for when I joined the exchange."

"You wanted to get laid, but not in public," she teased, but it was full of acceptance. I flushed and merely nodded at her. She was right. That was what I wanted before I met Ter-ak. My experience on Trillume kind of ruined things for me.

Violet plopped on the bed next to me and then stretched out, unconcerned with her state of undress. She was like a cat reveling in the aftermath of a good dose of catnip. She couldn't get her mind off of the commander that had escorted us. I smiled. I was glad she was enjoying this. One of us should.

"I never did say thank you. You didn't have to come with me, and you might still be in trouble. What I mean to say is that I'm glad I'm not alone. Thank you," I confessed to her while keeping my eyes on the wall in front of me instead of ogling her chest.

"It was nothing. Don't worry about it. I didn't do it for you, and I've been more than compensated, if you ask me."

After a heavy silence, she sighed and continued, "I left Earth to get away from my past, from a guy, and...."

I could feel the tremble of her arm next to my thigh, and I reached out to place my hand on her shoulder for support. She was holding on to something heavy, and I felt like there was this string between us that tugged at my own heart. It was moments like these that bonded girlfriends for life.

After her personal confession, I felt guilty for not revealing anything of myself, but I didn't want to take away from her experience, either. Her story wasn't mine to tell, and I waited until her burdens were unloaded before I spoke again.

Violet bolted up, only to collapse against me. I squeezed her close and confirmed what she already knew. What we both already knew about the men of our past. It felt like a shared hurt as I said, "That wasn't love."

Tears absorbed into my shoulder as Violet cried. A strong woman, capable of walking around naked without shame, and taking a spike in the hand without crumbling.

As my head rested on hers, and I stroked her back in comforting strokes, I couldn't stop my mind from wandering to the way a warrior once told me, "You can be my eyes, and I can be your legs."

It hit a little different in the moment as I thought about what it meant to be someone's eyes or legs. I was probably overthinking it, but it made me think that it was okay to not always be the legs that are forced to stand and stay strong. Right now, a woman that was most definitely stronger than me was using me as her legs to hold her as she healed.

Me. The weak one, held someone else up.

It was in this moment that I decided I didn't need a mate—I needed her. Violet was mine. It was nothing sexual. It was just a bond I never knew I needed. With a smile, I kissed her head. It felt good being needed by someone, and that I could be her legs for a moment.

Chapter Twelve
Broma

"Your ormete are discolored," Romek said offhandedly like it was basic conversation to talk about something I didn't want to be discussing with a traitor. It's been over a Dan star since I could feel the ends of them, but even knowing that the ormete that had been reattached were nothing more than ornamental at this point didn't pain me as much as feeling the last bit of my bond with my mate disappear from absence.

It had been long enough without being around her that I knew I wouldn't be able to feel the warmth of knowing she was near, even if she was. I knew the day she left the Blue District by the way my ormete ached from the loss. It was like my every fiber rejected letting her go. The nerves were dying, and I could barely lift even the parts of my ormete that were closer to my skull.

"You should cut off the dead parts before it spreads," he offered unsolicited advice.

"After you, then," I goaded him. Being stuck in the same room with him was becoming unbearable. We haven't even been able to use the lav station to clean ourselves, and his smell was making my nose burn.

He sighed. "We both know there is only one cure for your condition. You need to let go of the mate bond. It's already been rejected by being away from her for too long. Either you cut off the rot of being rejected, or you need to be close to her again. And soon."

"Lucky for us, our confinement is up as soon as our current blood samples are cleared," I dismissed his concern for my well-being.

"You can just bond with her again; there's no need to cling so hard to a broken bond."

"As soon as I felt her leave, I knew I couldn't let go. She may not have my essence anymore by now, but as long as I keep the bond, then I'll know when I'm close to her again."

He lifted a brow.

We hadn't talked much, but knowing I'd be rid of him soon seemed to loosen my lips.

"You wouldn't recognize her otherwise?" His confusion turned into understanding. "You don't even know her name, do you..."

"There was only one name that matched the criteria available. Her name is Violet."

"I wouldn't say her name unless she has given it to you herself," he warned with his tainted trill beliefs.

"Good thing I'm not you, then. You'll be returning to AsunGor with me to re-earn your right to representing the unGor on Trillume. You'll have to prove your motivations are for AsunGor, and not the trill."

A bang sounded off from the lav station, that had both of our gazes staring at the door. I opened the door to see what we had both feared as a possibility. The garrant's skin was in a fleshy pile scattered around a purple creature that huffed and stared forward like it saw straight through me.

Romek hovered behind, before he pressed the button to close the door again.

"If we want to leave today, we won't open that door again," he advised.

"Sedation initiated," the AI announced. "Your results are still negative. You will be released to a representative shortly."

Wooziness made me slowly crouch to the floor as I watched Romek collapse onto the bed. The light above the lav station was blue for locked, and I swiveled to see the door that had been blue moments before towards the hallway turn red. Someone was coming for us.

I struggled to stay conscious to know who was on the other side of the door. To my relief, I saw the familiar eyes of Pheyal and Vaquel.

"You smell like shit," Vaquel joked, but he wasn't wrong.

"You said you wanted to verify his vitals, not mate with him," Pheyal teased back. Smelling a warrior ripe after an ordeal was considered an intimate experience.

I closed my eyes, but replied with a croak barely above a whisper as I yawned, "I've honored you with the first sniff."

Pheyal laughed and said, "Right you have. You're a bit more ripe than anticipated. The fact that either of us still has a nose at all is proof enough that we will be brothers beyond death."

"I haven't agreed to join his delegation—speak for yourself," Vaquel denied with a chuckle that spoke of the opposite truth. He risked his life for me, and as far as I was concerned, he was already my brother in delegation, but it wasn't a decision that was up to me.

"He's hanging on longer than expected," Pheyal said.

It was the AI that replied to him, "Yes, he seems to be fighting the sedation I gave him."

"You opened the door anyway," Vaquel noted.

"It isn't necessary for the unGor Broma to be sedated. Please confirm which of you will be transferring the unGor Romek to the arena. The other will be free to leave the Blue District with the commissioner."

Before I could ask what was happening, the heaviness inside took over.

'Don't leave,' I thought as my ormete ached for my mate.

"He's coming to," Vaquel stated.

"As expected of the Mad Commissioner Broma," Pheyal said with pride.

"Mad is an understatement," Vaquel grumbled. "He should know how much it cost to program the nanomeds to stop his ormete from falling out after all the effort I made to fix them to begin with."

"Based on the way he's tensed up from your statement, it seems he already knows."

"What have you done?" I demanded.

"You will bond again," Pheyal assured. "We are already catching up to the necia ship as we speak."

"And she'll appreciate that you don't smell like rot," Vaquel added.

I groaned as I sat up, and the clear absence of her essence was disturbingly pain free. They'd made me sleep through the worst of it.

"I've never seen anyone hang on to a rejected bond so long when you can simply try again." Vaquel didn't understand.

"I thought you had mated with a trill?" He should know.

"Do not remind him," Pheyal warned, but I had already noticed the way Vaquel turned his attention fastidiously to arranging vials that did not need arranging.

He grumbled, "She was promised that I was someone I was not, with a title that I did not hold."

"I'm sorry." And I truly was, because it seemed by his response that he had liked her before knowing this and losing her. I would have welcomed any mate that brought him joy into my delegation. "Will you pursue it again?"

He shook his head to the negative. "I was infatuated with my own imagination. She was merely the current vessel for it."

Is that what I felt for my mate? Was I under an illusion of sharing a bond? She did leave when I was clear that we were mates, and that I had every intention of claiming her contract. Perhaps it was one sided? I would soon find out.

"How close are we?"

Pheyal eyed me curiously, and I realized I had instinctively reached for the empty space at my neck. I did not think it was possible to still feel such a pull when the bond was severed so soon, but I craved to be marked by her.

"You have a contract with her. There is time to bond again," Pheyal reasoned, but the long drag of his muscles showed he too understood losing the bond like I have means I no longer held a binding agreement with my mate that was enforceable by unGor law.

By unGor law, if I had held on to the bond in my own body, then my mate was required to reject or accept my claims after I've performed a ceremony of Gengaktor to prove myself. It would have been easy to find her by the warmth in my chest and the glow of my ormete, regardless of my ability to see her features.

Vaquel was less diplomatic in his words, and said what all of us were thinking, "A contract means nothing." He paused, considering the situation, and then his ormete twitched like they were shocking his mind into action. "Unless..."

"Unless what?" Pheyal urged for him to continue as I leaned in like his words would be the spring of new hope after a windstorm.

"Unless we can prove she didn't leave you by choice," he finally breathed out.

My shoulders sagged at this realization.

Pheyal shook his head and queued up a video surveillance. I watched as a group of new human arrivals on Trillume departed, one after the other, with their hosts. Two humans remained, waiting for some time together; neither of them showed signs of distress, or made any action towards requesting assistance from the trill security.

Then they were approached by a necia warrior—one of great honored standing in their tribe— who escorted them without any force. In fact, the warrior seemed reluctant to be there at all, even arguing with the human whose hair resembled red-colored ormete.

"Hope," I said.

"It isn't enough," Pheyal admitted. "By all appearances, the exchange was voluntary, and both humans left of their own choice."

"Which one is my mate?"

It wasn't like I could tell by an image alone without being around her in the flesh.

"The red-ormete, they call it hair."

But as the image froze, I tried to get a better look at the shorter human, who seemed to hide behind the other.

"And the black-ormete?" I questioned.

"Contracted with the necia warriors for a Rakture ceremony upon arrival. You should prepare yourself for the possibility that your mate has bonded with one of the necia warriors on the ship already."

I growled involuntarily, like my whole being rejected the idea of not being the first to mate with her. Calming myself, I replied,

"As the future primary delegate of AsunGor, she has the right to choose who she mates with..."

"And if she's already with offspring?" Vaquel interjected with his usual pessimism and yet very possible assumptions.

"Then we will raise the offspring and make sure we convince her mate to leave his tribe for a new one within her delegation," I said through clenched teeth. It would not be ideal. My brother would use that situation to try to take control of AsunGor. The first born of the Commissioner's delegation isn't even the commissioner's blood. It would not go over well with the clans.

"You wouldn't be able to give her first offspring the honor of your title..." Vaquel lamented with a sadness we all felt. We all knew that I would love the offspring as if it was my own blood and then politics would make us all choose between what was right and what was safest for the youngling.

I felt their whole life flash before my eyes and watched in my mind as Vaquel doted on a child with epul spikes that he trained to use while swimming in the caverns for their first hunt. I watched as Pheyal made him study how to manage a clan for them to one day take over the responsibilities.

I watched as an offspring not even born yet ran into their mother's arms, but from behind all I saw were shadows, forcing me to reach out and feel with my hands the silky hairs of her ormete. My hand, as it cupped her cheek and felt the way her mouth, turned up in a smile meant only for me.

"We will accept whatever happiness we are given," I confirmed out loud what my heart already knew. "I will speak with the commander and explain her importance beyond a contract."

"The necia warriors are territorial once they've mated," Pheyal warned.

Vaquel added, "I've researched the necia on board the vessel while you were sleeping."

"It wasn't exactly a relaxing rest," I objected, his tone like I had chosen to shirk my duties. "Nor was it a choice."

"I obtained the information," Pheyal corrected.

"While aboard the vessel--"

I cut them both off, "I know necia tribal law. If they are mated, then their laws while on a Galactic Authority vessel, or on their planet, will override any contract we have. Any of the warriors could try to mate with her to claim tribal law. We would have to negotiate for her to become the primary delegate of AsunGor."

Vaquel shook his head. "Or find a new mate."

"No," I objected, more harshly than I intended.

"There is something else you should know," Pheyal said calmly, but obviously concerned, "A highly honored warrior, second to the king of the House of Nel, is on board the ship."

"And?"

"He was contracted to mate with the other human... but..."

"A warrior off his inhibitors, intending to mate, may imprint on any potential mate..." I finished for him. It was my job as commissioner to know about the culture of many species to negotiate with them. "And you didn't think to mention this earlier?" I deadpanned. It was difficult to anger me, but this information was upsetting in a way that was irreparable.

A highly ranked necia warrior so close to the king of their planet would not be swayed to leave the tribe and join a delegation of AsunGor.

If my mate bonded with the Second of Necias Prime W ren-Kal... I would have no chance of keeping her. Thoughts of kidnapping her, simply grabbing her and waiting for her to forgive me plagued my mind. It would destroy my title, my planet's standing with Trillume, and with Necias Prime. I'd be putting us both in danger.

As long as she was happy, I repeated to myself over and over again.

"He's got that look in his eyes," Vaquel grumbled to Pheyal.

"You are not allowed to step down for your brother to take commission," Pheyal warned. "I would kill him in a duel, and we both know you do not wish for his death."

Many would die.

"If she is unhappy... I cannot make any promises," I admitted that I would destroy everything for a mate I hardly knew.

Vaquel didn't understand. "What is it about her that you can't let go of?"

"In the beginning, she was simply a human that was convenient and fulfilled a political purpose."

"And then?"

My thumb rubbed the grooves of the scar I held for her when I attacked the trill.

"She was attacked, and yet she cared for what would happen to the trill, and if he would die. Her sweet voice broke when she asked if I would die because I took on her burden of harming a male that did not honor her. There are wounds in her that are not seen. I could feel them as my eyes were covered in sap. She would delegate well with her softness and heal wounds others are blind to."

"You felt a softness in her?" Vaquel tried to absorb my meaning, but I could sense it would not be enough for him. He would have to experience it himself.

"She thought beyond my physical health to my future health as her concern extended to the consequences I might have for harming a trill diplomat," I continued.

"She sounds like a capable delegate," Pheyal agreed.

"I offered to kill the trill," I went on. "She did not wish for his death."

"Merciful," Pheyal mused and began to pace with his thoughts.

"She wished to know my failures..."

Vaquel took a sharp inhale at that confession.

"You did not..." Pheyal tensed as he gripped the dash of the control room panel to steady himself.

"I did not," I confirmed. "But she knew not all my scars were honorable, and she still wished to know more about our species. She still gave her consent. She displayed her tongue to me a third time..."

My heart raced at the memory—though I could not see her tongue, I could hear the way her mouth parted, and the little moan her throat made as she pushed her tongue before it licked across her lips.

"But the sap?" Vaquel was intrigued by this contrary statement.

"You could not see this," Pheyal agreed.

"I expressed that displaying her tongue would give me permission to show her what I could do with mine," I explained, and a shiver worked its way up my spine, tingling at my shoulder from the memory of her tongue caressing the very spot I wished for a mate mark. "She licked my neck."

"Near the shoulder?" Pheyal questioned, his eyes darting to the spot all unGor saved for their mate. It was the one spot where even if we had a scar there, we would insist a healer would take care to reduce scarring, or even risk nanomeds to protect.

With a sad smile, I admitted why I was so set on my mate. "She asked me what forever would be. She asked me what I would give her."

"What did you say?" It was Pheyal who whispered like he didn't want the universe to take back what it offered AsunGor when it brought our mate to me.

"I promised everything."

And I meant it.

Chapter Thirteen

Evie

It was entertaining living through Violet's romance vicariously. Watching the way she gravitated towards him, and even the way Mier-Lo reacted because of it. I wasn't sure why, but even after she had harmed Violet's hand, I should have been furious with her, but I couldn't bring myself to stay angry with her. Based on what I could observe, it wasn't a competition at all, and Mier-Lo held too much honor to accept a mate that didn't choose her first.

Not that I haven't called her a bitch in solidarity under the soundproof walls of my shared room with Violet.

I could respect Mier-Lo and choose to side with Violet, whatever her decision would be, but things changed when I heard the medic Ul-Ro say that Violet didn't stand down to Mier-Lo's challenge.

"You what?" I choked out, but no one chose to hear me. I stared at Violet, stunned, as she stood before me, yet again naked from her clothes being shredded to bits. She did have a cloak on from the medic, but she tossed it back at him, not wanting to owe him anything, or give him more reason to think she approved of his interest in her. I could tell by the way he gazed longingly at her that he was interested in her.

It didn't hurt that he was direct and also stated point blank that he wished to make her his mate, and not simply rut with her.

Violet had challenged Mier-Lo and didn't die... I whimpered at the knowledge that she could have, and it would have meant I was wrong about Mier-Lo's honor, or being deserving of my respect. It felt like such a stab to my trust, because she had been kind to me on multiple occasions when Violet was distracted with Commander Roe-el.

I wanted to fling my arms around Violet's shoulders to make sure she was real and in-tact.

Then Ul-Ro said, "There seems to be a vessel seeking to board our ship. You both should stay safe in your room until they leave. Some species are not as honorable as necia warriors. They are often associated with outlaws, capable of using those connections to avoid being accountable for stealing you to their planet, where their laws can protect them. I must return to the medbay in case of an emergency," he quickly added the last part as he rushed to leave, but not before turning to make sure we entered the room. "Do not leave your room," he warned again.

I shut the door and pressed the lock button immediately, taking the warning seriously. As soon as the metal was securely in place, I took a relieved breath before turning on Violet.

"You had a claiming ceremony?"

"If you mean we fucked, then yes."

I blushed and tried to not be upset that she didn't have time to tell me it was getting that serious with the commander. "How was it?"

"It was everything," she explained in delicious detail about how she felt seen until Meir-Lo tried to interrupt them.

Everything... I thought with jealousy. I'd heard that word before, and it was hard to hear anything past it as I watched Violet smile with such pure joy.

I forced myself to return to the present.

"And it didn't hurt?" I couldn't let my feelings get in the way of supporting her in her excitement. She jolted upright on the bed with a squeal.

"I came multiple times," she said with a moan. "I was building on another before I found out he was going to do more than cum... he was going to give me his mating seed."

I could tell by the way she said it, that there was more to it, and based on what Bode said about necia warriors, a mating seed was a bond you couldn't take back.

"And that's a bad thing?" I tried to be understanding. I couldn't tell which part was bothering her at first. Was it because she didn't want him to be her mate, or was it because he didn't ask her first? Or both? I gave her a gentle smile and sat beside her on the bed.

"No... yes. I mean, no. It is what I want, and that's what scares the fuck out of me. Literally, I stopped us, mid-fuck." She groaned with frustration at herself. I nodded as she continued, "What if this is just some pheromone-induced hysteria? What if humans weren't meant to mate with aliens? I mean, other than to have a bit of fun... What if our bodies can't handle a half-lethal-weapon of a hybrid baby warrior to term? We can hardly carry our own regular human babies!"

My eyes watered, but I didn't want to assume anything. I kept my breathing measured, so I didn't start imagining a little warrior human running around with red hair that would run into my arms with a giggle. I nearly choked right there. I could see it so clearly.

Then I heard his voice in my mind, "Everything."

I snapped out of it when Violet bounced off of the bed on her way to pacing the room in a panic. "I don't know! Yes." She grabbed at her hair and shook her head. "No." Groaning, she corrected herself, "Maybe?"

I patted the bed for her to return to my side for her to confess her darkest feelings of betrayal from the past, and I had to ask, "Did he force you?"

"No, he wanted me to choose him. He's nothing like my ex."

Tears flowed between us as I held her.

"Shhh," I comforted. "Sometimes things happen for a reason. You came with me when you didn't have to. When I needed you." And I was here for her when she needed me, I thought while I pet her hair and pulled it back from falling in front of her face.

"I've been a horrible friend," she sniffled with a hiccup. "I wasn't helping you. I was heat seeking an alien cock to fuck. He was cute, and I wanted him."

"You'd have come even without a sexy alien cock luring you in," I assured her with a smile.

"I'm not so sure."

"I am," I said with pep, forcing myself not to think about why Violet was feeling this way at all. It was my fault. I thought what she needed from me was my ears, but maybe I should have been more open with her about my own past. She was vulnerable with me, and I had yet to give her the same from myself.

Violet was willing to kick anyone's alien balls for looking at me sideways, regardless of if she would fuck them afterwards.

"You're the kind of person who sticks up for people, even if it means getting stabbed in the hand." I sighed, rubbing my face. "You took an epul thorn for me, you defended me, you told me your secrets, and I've told you nothing about myself. I'm so sorry," I said with a sob. "This is all my fault."

Folding over into my hands to cover my shame, I couldn't stop the tears as my shoulders shook from disappointment in myself.

Violet wrapped me up into her arms and patted my shoulder awkwardly with her hand. "I'm a fucking intimidating person. I didn't really give you the space to open up with all my own shit going on."

I sighed. "I guess we're both to blame." But I didn't think she had anything to be blamed for. I still felt incredibly responsible.

"Woah," she balked and pulled back, holding both my shoulders to make me look at her. "I wouldn't go that far. I'm pretty fucking awesome. Haven't you heard about that one time I got stabbed protecting a girl?"

A laugh escaped as I hiccupped from sobbing at the same time. "I think I heard something about that," I joked back.

"When you're ready, you can tell me more about what's been bothering you. Maybe when we're settled on Necias Prime?"

I took a deep breath. I could do this. Just say it. This whole ordeal was more than just a botched mate match with Trillume...

"It was never only about adventure," I started simple. I wasn't ready to talk about everything yet, but I'd start here. "I was going to age out of my housing."

"Oh shit," she said before clamping her hands over her mouth to let me keep talking.

"I found out that most of the contracts were mating contracts for a fertility research facility on Trillume. Every contract has a termination clause that acts as a failsafe for humans to breed with different species. It's why so many contracted exchanges never return to Earth. I've triggered my termination clause," I hesitated here but pushed on when she leaned in, biting her lip to stop herself from saying anything just yet, "Once the termination clause is active, any alien has a right to claim the contract for themselves, with none of the safety checks intended to protect our rights. All it takes is claiming they've bonded with me and I'd be forced to be their pet regardless of whether I want to mate with them or not."

"Wait," she tried to wrap her head around this, "Are you saying your contract with the necia isn't the original agreement? Fuck, no wonder you were terrified." She ran her hands through her red hair with worry. "You agreed to this?" Her eyes pleaded with me to say that I was okay with being here with her. She was so committed to staying with the necia now, that it would break her if I said no.

"Yes," I lied. "This is why I didn't say anything before," I watched as she stressed out about whether her choice to be with Roe-el was real or fake. Was she being manipulated, or was she in love? Those were things I couldn't answer for her. "I've always wanted a family," I tried to change the subject a bit, "My mom barely survived giving birth to me. It's true humans have a tough time with conception, even with other humans."

"Evie..." she said my name with pity. She already understood where this conversation was headed.

"Aliens don't offer the medical advances to humans without them joining the exchange. I'm okay with my family being half alien, as long as I can have one."

"Thank you for telling me." Violet rushed out her words and pulled me in for a hug, kissing my head as she cradled me close. I didn't even care that she was naked, and neither did she.

"I'm scared," I admitted. "What if I don't like the warrior that agreed to mate with me?" What if he tries to hurt me? I thought about Ter-ak. Then I thought about the unGor that I'd never see again. I couldn't tell her how sad I was when Medic Ul-Ro had told me I wasn't pregnant. It was only one night, and he was gone, but there was this pain in my gut when we launched into space that didn't feel like travel sickness. I wasn't sure, even with alien medical advancements, I was capable of having a child. The thought was devastating.

"I think it's entirely possible, and I look forward to being an aunty one day," Violet said while giving me a squeeze.

Was she saying what I thought she was saying? Being an aunty one day would mean that she'd be around long enough to see me find my own mate.

"Really?"

"You weren't planning on ditching me, were you?" she teased.

"I just didn't think..."

"You didn't think," she cut me off, "is right. I'm not going anywhere. It's you and me together, and I can't wait to see you get fat and plump with an alien spawn."

I chuckled and wiped at my eyes. She had a way of making me smile. "Thank you."

"We are family now, and I'll make sure you find your baby daddy, or protect you from one you don't want. Either way, I got your back, and I hope Roe-el has mine," she said with an exhausted sigh.

"You're going to tell him how you feel?" I asked.

"I'll sneak out after I take a nap. I'm exhausted. Who knew orgasms took so much energy?" she joked, like she usually did when she was avoiding something serious.

"Violet..."

"Yeah?"

"I look forward to being an aunty for you one day too," I confessed and squeaked as she pulled me into her chest to fall asleep.

Violet yawned and snuggled in. "We'll get fat together," she agreed. "That way, our kids won't be alone either."

"You think so?" It was a strange concept to think we could be moms together. Given all the evidence to the contrary about my fertility, her words made me hopeful in spite of it all.

"Only one way to find out, and the ride is worth the try," she joked, and I smiled, thinking about the one night I did try.

Soft breathing told me Violet was already asleep. I cringed as my stomach grumbled. I'd been avoiding leaving my room for the most part, and I'd probably already have starved if it weren't for Chief Wren-Kal dropping off food.

It was disappointing to force myself to extract myself from the tangle of Violet's arms and legs, but she was out cold, and I needed something to stop the gurgling in my gut. I didn't have to go far. Chief Wren-Kal was already waiting for me outside the room.

I shifted uncomfortably and turned my face away from him, but that didn't stop him from noticing the little things I tried to hide.

"You've been crying," he stated bluntly. A tray of food this time, instead of a squeezable mystery taffy.

"Is that real food?" I questioned with excitement.

"You've finished the microbe treatment, so your body should handle the change in food for common parasites in Necias Prime's offerings." But he wasn't deterred by my fascination with the food; he pulled it back before I could grab for the tray.

My mouth was salivating for something that didn't taste like cardboard.

"What has upset you? Were you told of the unGor boarding our ship?" he seemed upset himself with even asking the question.

"I was told," I confessed, but that didn't have anything to do with the emotions I was feeling.

"And you still came out of your room with no escort? Have you no instinct for your life?" he demanded, making his shoulder spikes flex with agitation.

"I don't see how that's any—"

"Concern of mine?" he finished for me. This was the first time I've ever seen him lose his composure. I took a step back, not from fear of him, but from realizing that if he was upset, then whoever was boarding our ship concerned him greatly. "As Chief of Security, anything on this ship is my concern. Do you see me delivering food to every warrior on this ship, Evie? Am I Chief of the Food Dispensary?"

"No..." I replied back with a tremble, still feeling emotionally charged from my chat with Violet. My eyes welled up again at being yelled at. I felt like such a child.

"You are a concern of mine," Wren-Kal said more gently, seeing how vulnerable I was. "I admit, I'm not used to struggling for someone's approval."

"My approval?" I squeaked, wiping at my eyes.

"I see no other female in the hall, My Evie."

Yours, I thought with a blush, before I cleared my throat to avoid acknowledging what he was saying.

"I've submitted a request with Medic Ul-Ro to stop my inhibitors and offer you my blood."

"You what?"

"I will rut for you. I request an offering of your blood or ellopul, so that I may hunt for you."

I coughed on my own spit at his directness. This whole time he had been so respectful of giving me space, and this was a drastic shift.

"Why now?"

"The unGor do not respect contracts that are not made in action. A contract is simply a document of intentions. Our mating arrangement would not be seen as binding by their species unless we establish a bond. With them going out of their way to track down our ship and board us, I do not believe it is without an intention to take what is not theirs.

"I was hoping to give you plenty of time to get to know me outside of the tribe and do a proper Rakture Ceremony when you were ready."

"I don't understand..." What was he saying?

"I am your intended mate," he clarified.

"But your brother..."

"We call many of our tribe brothers, regardless of ancestry, but I was speaking of myself. I am the second to the king and previous Commander of the House of Nel. And you, Evie of Earth, are my mate."

"Oh," I squeaked and rushed back into my room with my heart hammering in my chest. This was the opposite of keeping a low profile.

Chief Wren-Kal was very considerate, I thought with confusion. He was attractive, smart, kind, and just told me to give him a sample of my blood so he could hunt me down to... fuck me.

Oh, fuck...

Chapter Fourteen

Broma

Immediately upon boarding the ship and being greeted by the Commander, I knew. It was so obvious with the way he glowed and the smell about him. He was utterly satiated, having bathed in the juices of his mating. Was this what she smelled like mixed with another mate? I sniffed the air, and my nose wrinkled.

Was this jealousy?

It was an unusual feeling, considering I had accepted when I boarded that it would have been a possibility that she had found someone. I should be relieved that who she chose was not their Chief of Security; that would have ended any negotiations I could have made for her. Why was the second to the king of Necias Prime hiding out as the Chief? I'd have to hold off on my curiosity for now.

My request to see Violet immediately was denied, and I stood across from Commander Roe-el, awaiting her arrival for a shared meal. All of my hopes were resting on her recognizing me, even if she'd never seen my eyes. I made sure that my robes were cut so the sleeves would show off my scars, particularly that she could see the one I saved from our first meeting, and the bare space at my shoulder that I expected her to fill.

Commander Roe-el grumbled some pleasantries he didn't prefer to say but wished to express his disinterest in my presence all the same. "And you're the commissioner of what clan on AsunGor?"

I smiled at him and replied graciously, "The whole of AsunGor."

"You don't look female to me," he jibbed, obviously referring to his knowledge of my mother being the Commissioner of AsunGor.

I ignored his disregard for my title, unbelieving of my status. He would hear the stories of my accomplishments in time. "I suppose we have some things to discuss before she arrives."

"Humans do not track the time of sustenance at the usual universal star rotations," he agreed with the unusual lateness of the females to greeting us. I was fairly certain this wasn't a fault of the humans, but of his delivery of the information. It didn't serve a purpose to point this out to him other than being petty, so I continued without the interjection.

"In my time since last we spoke, I've been informed that you've claimed my delegate, exposing her to most of your tribe. Honored as I am that for your species it is a gesture of great respect—and shows how valuable you deem her worth—I ask that you refrain from showing any more signs of honor towards her. She is to be Delegate of Estate on the planet of AsunGor. As such, she is not to be touched by anyone outside of her delegation, such as a commissioner. You understand," I told him tightly through clenched teeth. It was difficult to keep my wits about me, knowing that it was this male that stood between me and my mate. Based on his stance on the other side of the table of untouched food, I knew he had no intentions of letting any other male near her.

Necia warriors may love to show off their mates, but they were not ones to share after bonding. A sudden realization struck me as I watched how tense he was. He was not fully mated to her yet. He couldn't be, or he'd be happy to show me his mate and flaunt how he can give her everything she needs. Including his cock right before my eyes. He'd make me watch as he fucked her, just so he could taunt me with his victory.

My smile grew larger. She hasn't accepted him yet. And I had no problems with her having her fun with a highly ranked warrior. If anything, her attachment to him only proves that she is perfect for being an AsunGor Delegate of Estate. Perhaps I could bond with this male and show him I only mean to bring our mate happiness. There is no reason we couldn't be part of the same delegation as long as he chose to step down as Commander.

"You must have her permission," he gritted back, "And as far as I can tell, she hasn't given it to you."

"I think there's a misunderstanding, Commander," I assured him, now more confident in my position to bargain with him. "I was already given permission when she signed the exchange contract. It was clearly marked as a permanent placement, as well as explained in detail in our contract what it meant to be an AsunGor Delegate."

Commander Roe-el slammed his fist on the table, fuming with rage. "You will respect her decision, whether it agrees with your contract or not!"

In that, we agreed. I laughed at how serious he was about making sure I abided by Violet's wishes, when this whole meeting was to set the stage so that she could truly have that option of finishing what we started on Trillume together. She would come with me. I knew it in my ormete as they warmed pleasantly ever since I arrived aboard the vessel. She was here.

I needed to make sure that this warrior wouldn't keep her against her will; that my contract gave her the ability to leave him.

"I have read the contract in detail, Commander. I have the permission of the Trillume Council and will provide for her—in every way. Emotionally and physically. Or did you think humans were simple creatures that you can fuck, and that was all there was to it?"

It was no secret that many necia warriors saw humans as pets, and I could not have the future Delegate of AsunGor, my mate, be disrespected as such.

"I know what necia warriors think of humans, Commander." I couldn't contain my vitriol about the subject of anyone thinking about my mate in this way, "Pets." I practically seethed before composing myself as my mother had taught me to in all diplomatic endeavors. "Fragile creatures, deserving of your protection, but not your honor or respect. You think Violet will choose you?"

He returned my calculating stare with one of cold resolve that was capable of frightening most males, but the more pissed he was, the more I knew I'd hit a nerve with him. That there was a truth he couldn't deny of himself.

I continued as his fist clenched at the table of our cold food. "Can you honestly say you cared enough to want more than slaking your cock's needs? Honestly, Commander..." I clucked my tongue in disappointment at the way his shoulders sagged despite the full display of his territorial epul spikes. "I thought you rose the ranks with intelligence, not brawn."

He was silent.

And that was telling enough.

"Good evening, Commander," a seductive voice called from the door. She was dressed in a gauzy, see-through gown that showed off everything I never got to see during our first encounter, and she was something much more fierce than I had anticipated. Her fiery hair was braided around her crown, practically matching the way the necia warrior had his own epul spikes protruding from his forehead and down his neck.

She was stunning, and on full display for both of us. This one action changed my whole perspective. She was wearing a mating robe. Most unGor would not know what they were looking at, but it was my job to know these things. I had to accept that Commander Roe-el was a package deal to have her as my mate.

"Who's the plus one?" she was narrowing her eyes at me. I was the intruder to her, and not an ounce of recognition was in those eyes for what we shared together. "Mier-Lo said you wanted to discuss my engagement..."

"To me," I corrected her and cleared my throat at the implications of what her original intentions were. I had to remain diplomatic. I had to remain calm. I could fix this. I had to fix this.

"You are stunning this evening, Violet," I said with a formal bow before introducing myself officially. "I am Commissioner Broma of AsunGor, with whom you've contracted an engagement my people call delegation. To humans, I believe it is correctly termed as marriage." I lifted my hand to her as I didn't think she'd appreciate being offered my ormete when her first mate of choice watched us. I had yet to come to a bonding agreement with either of them, and I was most assuredly the third wheel at this point.

This was not optimal.

She denied me the honor of touching her own hand, and I watched on as she paced the table in annoyance.

"Oh, fuck," she groaned. "Beth mentioned something about how serious it was, but I thought she was talking about being too hasty to leave on the next shuttle outta there. Read the fine print she begged me, but honestly, Bro-whatever, as nice of an offer as that sounds... I didn't read a single word of my contract. I thought all contracts were the same. You know, typical stuff like one-year terms, expenses covered, stipends, and all that. I didn't sign up for marriage."

Commander Roe-el growled like that was an affront to him while she wore the ceremonial robes of his tribe. She folded her arms over her chest, ignoring the outburst, and he seemed to understand that she was not discussing the lack of interest in him, but of myself.

He used my own words against me as he said with pride and mocking, "It seems there has been a misunderstanding, and Violet does not accept your contract of delegation. As you agreed, Commissioner, you will not take her against her will. She must willingly give permission to depart with you."

I nodded, but I had to know for certain she understood AsunGor did not have an issue with her keeping her necia mate if it brought her happiness.

"Violet," I tried to keep the hurt out of my voice, but it was difficult. "I've gathered honorable warriors who would love to learn from you and will follow your every command on ways to improve our planet with your soft and merciful ways to keep peace between our clans, as well as other planets. I've read your file and know what it would mean to you to fulfill your dreams. You will lead more than just your delegation, but a planet by my side. I promised you everything, and I intend to do that.

"I won't force you," I assured her with a sigh at the way she tensed up in my presence. "Whatever it is that brings you happiness, I vow to do everything in my power to assist its growth. It will take time, I know this, and I am a patient unGor."

My whole body quaked with what I could see was rejection in her eyes. I took my ormete in my hands, lifted it and bent to my knees before her in offering. Reluctantly, the Commander stepped aside for her to approach with my soul exposed and raw.

If Pheyal was here, he'd have demanded a duel with the Commander just to save me from the humiliation I was committing myself to. He would understand, but he would not want this rumor to spread of how I presented myself like this in front of any leadership. This was an action done in private meant only for a mate.

Her hand reached for her chest, and for a moment I thought perhaps I had swayed her, perhaps she had remembered me.

"Not that long ago, all of that would have made me ignore not knowing you. You tried to anticipate my every need, and you seem really devoted."

My ormete didn't glow or move from their dead weight in my hands. This was a rejection. She reached her hand out, but it wasn't for me.

With a commanding presence, she said with resolution, "I'm going to Necias Prime. I made a promise to Evie to look for loopholes in my contract because she didn't want me to deal with the termination clauses like she did, and because I wanted to stay with Roe-el. You know what I found, Commander?" Her focus was on her mate, eyes full of love.

"Necias's tribal laws supersede any contract while on Necias Prime, or any Necias operated ship where more than seventy percent of the crew are beholden to tribal law," Commander Roe-el finished for her. "As my mate, she is welcomed as a necia warrior and given all rights under tribal law."

She nodded at him, and I let my ormete drop to my shoulder while I stood to dust off my robes.

"Exactly," she chirped with excitement.

I smiled at them both and nodded my understanding, but a stubbornness took over that couldn't allow me to let my mate go.

"And you've consummated this bond, I assume?"

"Well, I was expecting to do that right now," Violet said while motioning to the obvious tribal mating gown. "Evie told me this is what mates wear when they are claimed. Do you like it?" She gushed at the Commander, who I could clearly see wasn't paying much attention to me any longer.

"I would have you if you were wearing Horve's great vines from the Forest of Thorns, but yes, you are a vision."

I cleared my throat to get back to my point. "I see there will be no changing your mind about the necia warrior, Violet. I will amend our contract to include the Commander, if it pleases you."

"What?" Violet replied in bafflement.

I repeated myself, but that did not seem to help, so I explained, "UnGor are not mated to a single commissioner, and there is no rule against multiple delegates." I winked at her, trying to win her over with what clearly was a more playful nature than I remembered. It was awkward for me to put on the charm, but I would do so for her.

"It is unusual for necia to pair with an unGor, but I can see he gives you happiness. I will do my best to accept him in our home. I had hoped to introduce you to a few of my brothers in delegation as options to acquaint yourself with more, but that can wait. If you would do me the honor of giving me your first born, I can accept Commander Roe-el as a brother in our delegation."

"Commissioner," Commander Roe-el stated firmly and with a tone that spoke of a coming duel, if I should refuse what he would say next, "a necia warrior does not share a mate." He paused and continued, "It is a common misconception to outside species, since we do what we must for our survival before we give our mating seed. Contrary to popular opinions, we only share the view, not the mate. We enjoy others knowing the beauty of our bond and the honor of our prowess at bringing happiness to our mates."

It was clear that he was exaggerating his politeness to get under my nerves and rub it in my wounds that unlike an unGor, he didn't need any assistance in keeping a mate happy by sharing a bond. I would not rise to the bait.

"Commander?" I added a note of curiosity to his title before dropping what my mother would call a political trap into his lap. "What happens to Violet when you return to your job?" If our past connection would not sway her, perhaps logic would. "You are a commander, are you not? You have duties to attend to that aren't simply escorting exchanges to their new homes, correct? Do you plan to stay on Necias Prime? Give up your honored position? Duel for leadership in your tribe? Or do you plan on continuing to command a vessel, dragging Violet around the galaxy?"

His mouth dropped open. He mocked my culture and customs in mating, but a delegation provided support for when one of us had to leave her for the good of the planet. The look of shock on Violet's face was enough to tell me that she, too, did not think of her future clearly enough. Though that was unlike her.

Surely, she had thought about it, and this was more the realization that her Commander was not giving up his career for her, and with me, that wouldn't be an issue.

After what was a rather lengthy pause that made the air heavy around us, Roe-el spoke. "I would follow where my mate goes. If she chooses to stay on Necias Prime, that is where I will find my place."

"And if she chooses to come to AsunGor?" I pressed the issue.

"She isn't," he snapped as she pulled her hand from his grip. I shook my head at the display.

I needed some space to think about things, and clearly, so did Violet.

"We have a few more days yet, before we reach Necias Prime. My vessel will follow, and I shall stay aboard the Mav Hel-le for the time being." I bowed to take my leave, exhausted from what was a meeting that did not go as my dreams had hoped for.

"Violet," I said while at the door. It opened for me, and I said my last remarks, "Consider that Commander Roe-el is a decorated warrior and has been assigned to missions classified so high, not even someone with my reach knows what he's up to when he isn't escorting beautiful women to their homes. He may wish to stay where you are, but he may end up dragging you where he needs to be or leaving you behind."

"Lies!" he barked as the door closed and reopened for me as I stood still.

"The unGor know that there is only so much one can accomplish on their own, and we accept brothers to assist where we cannot reach by ourselves. You will do well to recognize that what I'm offering both Violet and you, Commander Roe-el, is not an insult to your bond. When I accept a brother into my home, I seek to assist their happiness as much as my delegate's. Whatever that might look like for you."

I turned around to face him, and it was Violet who stood before me with her hand outstretched. There was a brightness about her, so I wasn't surprised at the way my ormete warmed suddenly.

"I only just accepted that I want this big brute over here, and I—"

She was interrupted by the door opening behind me again.

"Oh," a voice squeaked. "I thought you would be... you k now... in the claiming chambers now." Under her breath she grumbled about food, "It's probably cold now, and I'm so hungry. Awkward..."

I didn't dare turn around just yet. Warmth filled me at the sound of her voice. Roe-el turned with his epul surging with irritation at being interrupted again. I could understand that delaying a mating ceremony was difficult, but I felt the hairs on my skin prickle in an odd way that was uncomfortable. It was impossible that I was frightened of him. There were many other instances during our conversation where he was being much more intimidating. Violet smacked his stomach, and he retracted his epul, though I could tell that it was uncomfortable for him to do so.

I took Violet's other hand that was offered to me, hoping to feel the glow of our connection, but all I got was Roe-el's unpleasant territorial grunting.

I took a step to the side to make way for the new arrival and glanced between the two females with a smile. There was an affection there that warmed my heart.

"How pleasing to see you've chosen a sister delegate for yourself." I bowed to the other human, extending my hand. My breathing labored as I sniffed her skin, but I resolved to keep my composure. To hide my desire to lick her, exposing my tongue, I diverted to kissing for perhaps a second longer than appropriate atop her hand before releasing her.

"Violet?" her sweet voice questioned.

Then a heaviness consumed me as I saw another guest from behind her, ever the present reminder of his diligence. Chief Wren-Kal. He said nothing, but he didn't have to. His sights were set on the black-ormete human before me. His epul spikes were displayed territorially along the crown of his head.

Straightening, I knew this human would bring my mate happiness, and my confidence rose as I watched her lick her lips, exposing her tongue to me. My chest warmed at the sight.

"I am Broma, Commissioner of AsunGor. You are exquisite. I look forward to sharing our home with you." My voice vibrated with a mating call, that I had intended to only use when Violet chose to accept me. It was unintentional, and probably a result of being so close to her. I could only hope that the commander did not take offense to a tactic that he would find unsuitable for negotiations. If Roe-el is to be a brother in my home, I must show him respect.

My ormete lifted from my shoulder, and I quickly guided it as an offering to hide its movement. It was only further proof that I had indeed made the correct decision to board the ship and pursue my mate.

I couldn't take my eyes off the human as she hesitated to touch my ormete braid.

"Your hair is..." I wished to correct her and say hair was a human term, but the way her breathing quickened around me had me distracted, waiting for her to feel the vibration of my ormete with those soft fingers. She pulled back—to my disappointment—and cleared her throat. "...fascinating, but uh..."

She glanced back to Violet, seeking approval to be interacting with me. A very diplomatic gesture when faced with the uncertainty of the situation. It was a sign that she cared deeply for

Violet and did not wish to harm her with what I could smell on her as clear attraction to me. The smell was intoxicating.

Even Chief Wren-Kal's nostrils were flaring, and his muscles were straining to hold his position, guarding and watching the situation unfold.

"He's the one I signed a contract with," Violet explained, and I watched as the black-ormete silk shifted with the deflation of her shoulders. It was momentary, before she pepped up and smiled. A smile I knew all too well to tell the difference between happiness and obligation.

"Oh, right!" She chirped, before narrowing her eyes at me like I had done something in need of being reprimanded for. Even that look quickly adjusted to a widening of her eyes as they darted around the room with panicked anxiety. "Are you here to take Violet to AsunGor?" She was a human of many hidden emotions, I thought with curiosity. Was she upset with me, or excited that I was here?

Then suddenly, a surge of heat shocked through my system as her hands sprung to grasp my own. My ormete caressed the tops of her small hands with a slight glow.

"Please don't take her from me," she pleaded.

My heart swelled, and it was then that I realized my mistake. Violet was indeed important, and she had a lingering smell about her that spoke of close contact with my mate. It was this human's happiness that mattered most to me. I would do what I could to convince Violet to stay with my mate.

"I would never dream of separating you from someone that makes you happy," I assured her. Closing my hands around hers protectively, I lifted them to my cheek to feel the way she had touched me before, when I had no eyes to see her with. "What is your name, beautiful delegate?"

"Evie," she said with ragged breaths.

"I think that's enough, don't you?" Violet demanded. Reluctantly, I pulled away as Violet guided my mate from the room and past the looming presence of Chief Wren-Kal.

"Evie." I enjoyed the way her name flowed off my tongue and then smiled. She was hungry, and she came to this room for a reason. It might not have been for me, but it seemed everyone had not noticed the way she stared at the table with interest, or the way her stomach grumbled for sustenance.

"The food has grown cold," I motioned to the feast, wasted from Commander Roe-el's need to pretend he actually wanted either of the humans to meet with me. It was clear from the first words Violet spoke that she had only heard of the meeting because of the second in command, Mier-Lo. That information was curious, but not my priority at the moment.

"Shall we go fetch some more from the synthesizers?" I offered to Evie, and she stopped her strides in the hall.

This was a tricky situation I was in, politically. I had a contract with Violet, and it seemed my worst fear about Chief Wren-Kal was true. I had to navigate this with caution with a bit of misdirection, so it would be too late for them to avoid my new intentions.

"Violet," I addressed formally, "I will endeavor to bond with your sister while you take some time to think about our marriage."

It was not a lie. I did detest lying, but it wasn't entirely truthful, either. Diplomacy wasn't always a straight line.

"You don't have to do this," Violet held my mate protectively. This was a beautiful sight to me.

"Did you claim your mate yet?" Evie whispered, though she knew by the way her eyes assessed everyone, that it wasn't much of a secret with an unGor's hearing.

A small shake of Violet's head confirmed my own suspicions, and then Evie puffed out her chest and took a deep breath. "I'll give you some time. Don't worry, I'll be okay," she said while watching me. Of course, she knew I meant her no harm.

Then she glared, and there was a bite of irritation as she told me, "I already ate, but there is one more place the necia don't seem to show their 'honor' in, besides this room. Care to join me?"

How very diplomatic of her, I thought with interest. But I very much knew she was lying about having eaten, and did not wish for her to go hungry. This was not an ideal state to be trying to convince her to bond with me again.

"Wonderful," I kept my tone neutral, though I wished to express how excited I was to be alone with her. Were we to be alone? I turned to Violet, who had already moved to rejoin Commander Roe-el. "Violet, will you be joining us?"

"Actually, I'm famished," she said seductively to her mate.

Commander Roe-el spoke without taking his eyes from Violet to inform Evie that it was possible to see my ship from the observatory, and she's welcome to take a guard with her as an escort. It was his not-so-subtle way of reminding me that I would not be alone with Evie. And Chief Wren-Kal promptly stepped forward to offer his services.

As we exited, I prompted an inquiry into how much he's told my mate about himself. "It is an honor to be escorted by the Chief of Security," I nodded to him, my tone clear that it was unusual for a chief to be reduced to simple escort duty when there was a ship and crew to protect.

"You are lucky," he agreed. "The Mave He-el has two chiefs, as I am only temporarily assisting this ship until we reach Necias Prime."

She knows he will be returning to his previous title planet side, but does she know who he is?

He continued, seeing my curiosity, "Chief Ther-ol will remain on ship when we arrive, and I will stay with my mate as the second to my king."

His mate? "You are mated then?" I asked Evie with false pleasantry. It was difficult to keep my tone soft with her when I was feeling threatened by the warrior walking too close to her.

She huffed out with her own annoyance... at me?

"You're one to ask me that," she mumbled under her breath.

I had to speak carefully with Wren-Kal present. If he catches on to me wanting Evie instead of Violet, then it would be more difficult for me to do what Violet and Roe-el are currently doing to break our contract. Claiming tribal law was a tricky game. Though I didn't mind Violet ending our contract, but it wasn't something I could easily let go of without putting AsunGor's reputation at risk.

"I believe you'll feel more comfortable with my purpose for tracking this ship down once I tell you a story," I began.

"I thought the unGor didn't tell their own stories; they had to be earned," she said with a lift of her brow in challenge.

"Most correct, Evie of Earth." I made sure to have her association still be that of her home planet and watched as the chief's jaw twitched in irritation. To him, he would prefer to have her associated with Necias Prime, and if he were mated with her already, then he would have corrected me. This was good news. "The only stories I may tell are those of other honored warriors, and those of shared experiences. Often, an unGor will remind a mate of the scars they've earned to prove their devotion."

"Some scars will never be seen on your skin, Commissioner," she replied prettily enough, but there was a sharpness I felt dig deep.

I pressed on. "Mating scars are ones an unGor may boast to others without diminishing the experience—as many mating scars are not a public affair. I lifted my hand to show off the scraps of trill teeth around my wrist and fingers.

"This scar was earned saving my mate from a trill's poison. I dug my fist into the trill's mouth and pulled out its enzyme sack from behind its teeth. They use those enzymes to make their food safe to eat even after they poison their meat. Believe it or not, the trill may be resistant to their own poison, but it's more of a tolerance built up since their youth, and they still need the enzymes to break down the poison enough not to get sick themselves."

"I'd think the trill would want that information kept a secret," Evie said conspiratorially.

"It is not a widely known fact," I agreed. "Speaking of this around a trill would certainly give them reason to make you their next meal."

"This is not what I was told about how to cure trill poison," Chief interjected, relishing an opportunity to prove me wrong on something, but I was hoping he would try to make me look dishonorable in front of Evie.

"Ah, yes. You're probably referring to eating a trill's heart. If the sacks are damaged or have already been used up, then yes. The best you can do is eat their heart to absorb as much of their antibodies against the poison as you can. It's a rather lethal option, if you ask me."

The chief closed his mouth, not wishing to fall into another one of my traps, because I was enjoying the way Evie gave him a shocked look of disgust before she finally gave me the honor of her gaze. In those eyes I saw a kindness and understanding.

"You could have killed the trill by eating his heart to counteract the poison from your wound..." She added quickly after a moment of reflection, "In the story about saving your mate?"

"My mate did not wish for the trill to die," I explained. "I also have my belief that she did not wish for me to have more difficulties negotiating with the trill in the future either."

"You keep calling her your mate but left her to join the necia in your absence," she pointed out, and it was a clever statement that Chief Wren-Kal would not be certain wasn't about Violet. It was also very telling of why she had left me if she thought I had abandoned her first.

"Circumstances prevented me from claiming my mate earlier."

"Circumstances?" she questioned, wanting more information that I couldn't provide.

"I'm unable to discuss them at this time," I regretted to say.

"Of course you aren't," she snapped, and I heard her stomach grumble once more.

"As lovely as watching the stars from the observatory sounds, I must admit that I didn't have a single bite of the food from earlier. I prefer to eat after everyone else has had their fill, but now I'm certain waiting longer is not an option. Shall we grab a quick bite from my room's dispensary?"

"Your room has a dispensary?" she questioned in disbelief.

I nodded and proceeded to walk in the direction of the diplomatic suite. Every larger ship like this one had a room larger than even the commander's quarters for an occasion of having to host someone of my title and honor.

I was surprised, after hearing Chief Wren-Kal hadn't taken the position from Ther-Ol, that the diplomatic suite was available. Someone of his rank could have easily requested it for himself.

"I advise against returning to his room," Wren-Kal spoke up.

"He does not like the fact that it's the only room he's not allowed to enter without permission from the commander of the ship. As he does not have the commander's code, and the new protocols mean the code changes every time it's used once, that means he can't hack the room without informing the commander of his misuse of power, damaging his honor," I explained.

Wren-Kal growled, and his eyes turned black. That was a troubling sign of him potentially rutting soon. The necia were a volatile species when their instincts took over. They were supposed to be taking medication to prevent such instances, but I had a feeling he wasn't taking his anymore.

"You could just invite him in," she suggested, and I smiled between them both.

"The chief is well aware the invite was for you alone. He will surely keep watch outside the door to make sure I don't abscond with you to my ship."

"Would you do that?" she asked with wide eyes.

I chuckled. "Do you want me to?" I replied smoothly.

Her cheeks blushed pink, and I took that as a sign that it wasn't off the table of options. How interesting.

But first we had to take care of that hunger making her stomach threaten her with a roar loud enough to echo down the hall.

Chapter Fifteen
Evie

I didn't want to go to the cafeteria, and after what Wren-Kal said about wanting my blood offering for a rut, I was definitely safer in the one room he wasn't allowed to hack into with his security clearances.

"Ah," Broma got my attention while gesturing to the double sliding door at the end of the hall with two security warriors outside. "It seems I'm not the only one to return to the room. Vaquel and Pheyal's escorts are here as well."

"Who?" I asked.

"Commissioner Pheyal is a highly requested clan of Asun-Gor for many diplomatic resolutions across the galaxy. He himself has been responsible for negotiations with galactic troublemakers to keep their business from spreading unchecked. Many of his adornments have been achieved from dueling victories with many lethal species," he boasted. "Vaquel is his closest brother, and he is remarkable in his healing methods, having learned from several planets during his diplomatic visits. Both have serviced AsunGor long enough to settle into a delegation or select their own priorities of how to serve AsunGor in the future. They currently choose to support my commission."

"That is a fancy way of saying his warriors are retired," Chief Wren-Kal mused with a smirk.

"A concept many species should consider as an earned privilege sooner than they do," he considered thoughtfully, but I could hear the undertones of accusation that the necia warriors do not appreciate their warriors as well as they could. "On AsunGor," he addressed me conversationally, "we do not wait until our warriors age into elders to gain the honor of choice. Any warrior may choose a new path without losing his prior deeds of worth."

"Any warrior?" Wren-Kal questioned just as casually, but I could see this was some kind of pissing contest between them. "Does that apply to your offspring as well?"

I glanced between them both, not quite understanding what he was trying to insinuate, but for the first time during their verbal sparring, I saw Broma tense up. The smile he had been wearing up until then was tight, with his jaw flexing.

"No, I suppose the future brood of Commissioner of AsunGor would be required to duel for future leadership against every warrior that sought to claim the title for themselves by choice," Wren-Kal clarified for me, because there was no point in saying something out loud that they both knew the answer to. This whole conversation was for my benefit. A show.

"Your children wouldn't have a choice?" I asked him softly with concern.

"Commissioner Broma tried to abdicate his own title to his brother but was bound by his own laws to duel him," Wren-Kal explained, "He is called the Mad King because he cut his own brother's ormete at the root, then cut his own ormete off so he'd have no claim of retribution against him. An unGor willing to maim himself to make sure his own brother couldn't re-duel him for commission."

Broma turned away from me so I couldn't see his face and opened the door to his room without a word. My chest clenched on itself—feeling like what Wren-Kal had just recounted for him was a painful memory, or maybe that was just my way of rationalizing that he wasn't dangerous. That he wasn't as vicious as Wren-Kal made him out to be.

I rushed after him; the door shutting behind us before I could think clearly about following him into a room the security chief couldn't access without commander approval.

"Wait," I squeaked, reaching for him.

The most common assessment of that story would be the same as the people who called him the Mad King of AsunGor. That he was crazy enough to destroy himself just to make sure no one else would attempt doing it themselves. A proof of action that told everyone that there was nothing they could do to break him.

What about the fact that he was forced to duel his brother against his will? What if he was destroying himself as an attempt to leave a position that he had no intention of having? Only for it to fail, and be stuck leading his planet, anyway.

Which one were you, Broma of AsunGor?

"Why did you do it?" I finally asked.

He didn't turn to face me.

"My brother Brakaun has stated his desire to profit with pushing our agreements with outlaws that would bring with it risks I wasn't supportive of for the future of AsunGor, which included the acquisition of humans as breeding stock instead of mating with them."

Another deep voice cleared their throat to get my attention before adding, "Brakaun is not a bad unGor, but he is too inexperienced to know the consequences of his ideas."

Another male said, "His weapon was dipped in poison and if Broma hadn't redirected it... it could have permanently damaged his ormete because Brakaun wouldn't have given up the source so quickly to save himself."

"Poisoned?" I gasped. He used a poisoned blade on his brother and himself?

"Brakaun didn't want to risk Broma being able to take commission from him. Poisoning his ormete would destroy any chance of properly mating or being seen as a strong leader."

"But he didn't want it!" I defended like I knew Broma wasn't power hungry, just from a few meetings and conversations.

"Youth does not always know what it needs," the large unGor sitting at a table of what I now noticed was a very lavishly large suite said. One eye was slashed and milky, with a harsh scar.

"That is Commissioner Pheyal," Broma introduced. "His eye was lost when he killed a slaver keeping unGors in a milking farm to sell our seed for blue market fertility treatments. He set up voluntary farms on the planet for donations to trade the treatments ourselves. And over there is Vaquel; his ormete have been gifted with adornments from the patients whose lives he's saved."

"Gifted? You make it sound like I have not earned them," he grumbled.

"He prefers the term trophies of life, as one would call your trophies ones earned in death," Pheyal added casually about bones and metal braided through their hair. Ormete, I corrected myself. There were several strands thin enough to be considered similar to human hair, but I remembered how Broma described it as those many hairs bonding together to form the larger tentacles that hid braided underneath.

"And what would yours be called, then?" Broma asked, while selecting food options from the dispensary. "Did you sneak some fresh har fruit in your robes?" He asked Vaquel, the atmosphere of the room lighter than it had been moments before. There was an easy comfort between the un-Gor, and my presence didn't seem to disrupt that.

"Of course I did," Vaquel said with excitement as he lifted his robes to show a few large pockets bulging with a strange oval shaped rock spotted with blue. "They aren't as fun to eat when they ripen too much, though," he said while inspecting the speckled coloring.

"It seems the oils have leaked from the sacks to spot them," Pheyal agreed. "You were not careful in their transport."

"Of course not, they were in my pockets, bouncing about!" Vaquel defended like he shouldn't be held responsible for the "bruising" of the fruit, if that was what they were talking about? *Bruising usually made a fruit soft, but it wouldn't make it bad to eat*, I thought.

"It will still be sweet, and the smell is mostly a defense mechanism to prevent animals from eating it before the seeds have formed."

"The seeds are not digestible," Vaquel warned, giving me a shake of his head like I was a child, but to them I might as well be, since I didn't know much about their planet or their food. "But they are useful in poultice for healing when you break open the husk for the oil inside."

"I wonder how someone discovered that?" I accidentally said out loud.

Vaquel smiled and motioned for me to follow him to the table where Pheyal sat, and Broma was bringing a tray of food. He used a clawed thumb nail to cut the hard flesh of the fruit, then peeled it back carefully to expose the creamy fibers with blue veins. A pungent smell wafted up from the fruit and I wrinkled my nose. The whole table chuckled at my reaction.

"It is an unpleasant smell, but it is temporary. Wait a moment," Broma said while mimed holding the fruit to smell it.

"I'm not putting my nose in that," I objected.

Vaquel pushed a finger into the soft fruit and rubbed it before lifting it to my nose. I balked and jerked back, but he was faster and rubbed the juice under my nose. To my surprise, it was not foul smelling at all.

"The smell is foul because the juice sack has broken, but the juice is sweet, and when it's combined with the flesh, the smell neutralizes. It's most pungent when it's still absorbing into the flesh, but the enzymes in the flesh create a soft, but distinct smell similar to the tree it comes from."

"Woodsy?" I said and picked up the fruit.

"It's why when they get ripe like this, then we blend the fruit. But when blending, if any seeds have formed, they are harder than the skin and do not mix." Vaquel seemed pleased to see my interest in knowing more.

Broma added, "Our ancestors tried chewing, or swallowing the seeds whole, only to find the seed intact and making the digestive process unpleasant. But elders knew that seeds had to contain life in them to create a har fruit crop. So they watched the seed to see what would happen if they waited."

I was intrigued and leaned in while staring at the fruit on the table. Broma's voice was so deep and comforting that I could have listened to him talk about anything.

Broma stuck his fingers into the har fruit, rubbing back and forth until a blue seed pushed out. My breathing hitched as I watched him, and I chided myself for sexualizing a fruit like he could be rubbing my clit.

"Looks like this one had enough time to seed," he said, but Broma's eyes weren't on the fruit at all. They were watching me. I gulped and nodded for him to continue. "They found the seeds were shaped with these grooves that caught the wind just right to bury themselves into the ground like a drill, and the ones that didn't would soften enough to squeeze. The oil it gave was much too bitter to eat, which—"

Broma was cut off by the excitement of Vaquel. "The poultice was discovered because our ancient ancestor was pissed off at someone and wanted to ruin the taste of their meal. They added the oil to the lard, but instead of using that batch of lard for food, he was injured on the hunt and had to use it for plugging up the bleeding. A nephic shark has poison that prevents wounds from closing. The lard acts as putty to seal the wound, and instead of simply protecting the wound, the oil from the har seed burned the poison off, and the wound was healed the next rising, while leaving behind a blue tinge to the skin that some warriors like to use for coloring their scars."

"The elder became frustrated that his prank had made his rival the talk of the clan as being blessed for his rapid recovery, that he purposefully hunted to catch a nephic alive to repeat the wound by dueling him with a weapon dipped in nephic venom," Broma absently reached for his ormete braid and then cleared his throat to speedily finish the story, "Eventually, they figured out that it was the seed oil and both unGors united under the same delegation becoming brothers with great reputations for discovering a great use of har seeds." He took the har fruit and mushed up the flesh until it was a light blue paste with his fingers and then scooped it out. It no longer smelled weird, and he offered me a plate. "It will make the food more tolerable if you spread it on top like a jelly."

It was a jelly, I thought, considering it was simply smashed up fruit, but maybe they called that something different?

"Har jelly," I said while taking the offered plate. Hesitating, I confirmed with him, "The food isn't shit, is it?"

Bode had been quiet lately, and this time he answered in my implant, "It is likely many of the foods from a ship's food generator contain feces from various kinds of species, but your preferences state you do not wish to verify this information so I will say that most ships use molds filled with a mix of ingredients based on their last traveled location. Being as that was Trillume, and a recent shipment from Earth, you might be consuming Earth materials."

I smiled awkwardly. That didn't help.

"I find it easier to eat while traveling when I think about how one species's waste is another's snack," Broma said while liberally applying har jelly to my molded food. "The har fruit is also very good for digestion."

"Just not the seeds," I joked.

Pheyal laughed and patted Broma on the back. "A perfect delegate," he said with a smile, "one that will not agree to be agreeable, but will catch you when you miss a step. This is pleasing."

"A contest!" Pheyal proposed, grabbing a har fruit from Vaquel's hand.

"The har fruit is too ripe," Vaquel replied with disappointment.

"What kind of contest?" I asked, suddenly feeling my inner competitiveness rise to the occasion.

"One where you are the judge," Broma said before licking the har jelly from his fingers, his tongue slipping between the two suggestively, making me shiver.

"You're just going to let him bare his tongue at her like that?" Vaquel complained to Pheyal.

"Has she requested he not?" Pheyal dismissed his concern. The response was a scoff as he folded his arms over his chest; Vaquel's ormete seemed to quiver about his shoulders in annoyance, but also acceptance. At what I didn't know. Though, the last time Broma spoke of tongues, he made it seem like there was a whole law around the display of it, and the last time I did it... Well, I wasn't mad at what happened next.

"And what would I be judging for?" I prompted after they all watched me curiously.

"Eat," Broma insisted, nudging the plate closer, and taking a finger to the food to bring to his lips. He took a bite, sucking it off his finger, and assured, "It is safe. You'll need your energy for the contest."

I scooped up the food with my finger like he did and stuck my tongue out to lick it off, making him moan as he watched. His nostrils flared, and I remembered the way he was when we first met. And then I remembered the way he never returned, and I turned my cheek to him instead, looking at the wall.

"She is upset with you," Vaquel mused with a satisfied harrumph. "If we are playing for which of us will bond first, he will surely not make use of it."

"No, that is a contest for another time," Pheyal's deep voice rumbled. "We will perform a gen of finding."

"An unofficial Gengaktor trial?" Vaquel leaned forward, intrigued.

"How do you do a gen of finding?" I asked, still avoiding eye contact with Broma.

"It is simple," Pheyal replied with a smile. "But we will not do it without your permission. Often, a delegate's consent is implied as they are the host of a Gengaktor Ceremony, but as you do not know our culture, I've suggested it for you, and you need only agree."

Broma explained, "A gen of finding is a ritual of rubbing our scent on you, then the next rising, you will seek out which one of us you wish to give your scent to in return. This helps an unGor form a bond with you."

"How... how do you give your scent?"

Pheyal smiled, his canines extending like a predator.

"Evie," Broma begged for me to look at him with a sultry call of my name. "I gave you my scent the first time we met, and I would have wished to give it to you again if I was not detained by the Blue District's AI."

"Bode?"

"Confirmed," Bode spoke from my translator, "the unGor had been exposed to a viral contagion and was unable to be released for two Dan star rotations."

I gasped.

"You didn't leave..." I was putting the pieces together. "But, Violet?"

Pheyal spoke then, glancing between us, "I had searched for locally held contracts with humans that matched terminated mating contracts with a trill diplomat... there was only one available. Violet originally held a contract with a trill diplomat, only for it to suddenly be canceled for an immediate transfer request. It met the description of your meeting with Broma."

"Violet was still on Earth; she was in a hurry to leave a bad situation and wanted her exchange to happen sooner..." While my contract had transferred immediately from Ter-ak to the necia mating contract. "I never told you about the necia," I said out loud, understanding that I was the one who left.

I didn't realize how much hurt I held onto, thinking he left and how much rationalizing I forced myself to repeat to convince myself that I knew it was only a one-time thing.

"I can't cancel my delegation contract with Violet without having enough of a reason for the clans to support a stronger claim," Broma explained. "She needs to bond with her necia mate irrevocably, and I must repair our bond."

"Repair..."

Vaquel groaned. "He tried to fight the mating sickness, but I had to sever the bond to save him. Once an unGor bonds, they need continued contact with their mate to make the bond permanent, or they need to accept the rejection."

"Accept the rejection?"

"The bond was severed because I was kept apart from you for too long, but my ormete remember. If you accept the gen of finding, we can repair it."

"Tell her the risks," Vaquel urged.

"If you reject a second bonding..." Broma couldn't finish the thought.

"The bond will not be capable of repair," Pheyal said while pushing from the table and kneeling with his ormete braid presented to me. Vaquel followed his lead and lifted his ormete in offering.

Broma sat across from me, waving to the food tray. "Please finish. We will wait."

"You're not hungry?"

My stomach gurgled again, and I winced at the sound with embarrassment.

"We will wait," Broma repeated. "What we are hungry for is not on the plate."

My cheeks heated.

Broma grunted and jutted his chin at the other unGor. They nodded and stood. Pheyal dipped a finger in my food and offered that to me instead. Vaquel, not to be left out, dipped his finger in and nudged it closer to my lips for me to eat from his finger first.

Broma watched me to see what I would do.

Knowing that he hadn't left me and came halfway across the galaxy to catch up with me made me more brazen. I stared at Broma as I gently guided Vaquel's finger to my lips by his wrist.

Without breaking eye contact, I flicked my tongue up Vaquel's finger, scooping the food into my mouth.

Vaquel groaned. "Nnnng, fff-yesss," he said incoherently, with a shudder traveling up his arm.

Broma's eyes hooded with an intensity that challenged what I would do next. My heart was racing, and my blood rushed to my ears, pounding, as I placed my finger under Pheyal's hand. I didn't grab him, I merely moved my finger closer to my lips, and his hand followed as if magnetized.

His chest rose and fell rapidly as he watched me. So I paused, smelling the sweet, woodsy aroma of the har fruit jelly. Pheyal growled, but did not push his finger into my mouth, and my eyes never left Broma's.

"Show me your tongue a third time, my mate," Broma commanded as he undid the clasp holding his robe around his shoulders.

I opened my mouth, sticking my tongue out and licking up Pheyal's finger, before sucking off the food. They all watched me as I let it dissolve, and my throat bobbed as I swallowed. Self-conscious of what I'd just done to Pheyal and Vaquel's fingers while eye-fucking Broma, I suddenly felt very uncertain. My eyes went wide. What was I thinking?

"We will now offer our ormete," Pheyal said, and they all kneeled on either side of me, lifting their braids. Strands of silver hair glowed and lifted like they were caught in a gentle breeze.

I reached out my hand, and each of their ormetes floated up to wrap around my hand and wrist. My skin warmed at the contact.

"I, Commissioner Pheyal, offer my scent."

"I, Tactician Vaquel, offer my scent."

"I, Broma, Commissioner of AsunGor, offer my scent."

Warmth tingled up my nose, and my thighs clenched together. It became difficult to breathe, each inhale coming in shallow and rapid. With a twitch of my fingers, I caressed their smooth tentacles. They had their main ormete braided and decorated with bones and memories, but what wrapped around my wrist were unadorned tentacles.

I had to ask, my voice low and husky, "Where are your memories?"

"We're making them now, little delegate," Broma replied.

"There are ormete we save only for a mate," Pheyal explained.

"For her," Vaquel corrected Pheyal.

"For you," Broma confirmed, watching me squirm in my own skin.

"What is happening to me? I feel... I feel so..." I moaned and gripped their ormete tighter in my hand, my other hand reaching to run my fingers through Broma's strands.

"Do you wish for us to care for you?" His head leaned into my touch, and he closed his eyes with a moan that I echoed back as I rubbed my thighs together.

"She is reacting strongly to our scents," Pheyal said with a pleased grin.

Vaquel took a deep inhale and groaned. "She isn't the only one."

But I couldn't fall into his trap again without knowing what it meant to bond for an unGor.

"Bode," I tried to activate him with a rasp. "What happens to an unGor when they bond?"

Will he leave me again?"

"UnGor keep much of their planet's dynamics disconnected from technology, but according to much of my research, they have one primary delegate, considered similar to human marriage, but more than a contract. They can only obtain one bond, but that bond can grow if another unGor bonds with the same delegate, expanding their delegation with the approval of the delegate. Bonds are not immediate and must be maintained until fully matured or risk harming the unGor's health. Based on tracking news of Commissioner Trema's delegation, her mates were numbered in hundreds if we conclude that every clan had at least one commissioner sent to mate with her, and no records of her rejecting any of those offers."

"Hundreds?" I gasped.

"She seems to have connected with the Blue District database," Pheyal commented.

"She seems frightened," Vaquel added.

"We bond only once," Broma assured. "Only you are in charge of who we accept into your delegation. One cannot force a permanent bond, and you can reject a mate by denying them what they need to bond."

"What do you need?" I asked him.

"You."

My heart swelled with warmth and the air felt charged as my whole body begged to be touched.

"She's ready," Pheyal spoke deeply.

They all released their ormete from my hand, and I whimpered at the loss of contact with them as my body cooled with their absence. I shivered.

My vision went fuzzy and their voices seemed to echo in my head.

"I always imagined we'd do this on AsunGor," Vaquel said, breathing heavy.

"We won't be able to leave this ship without her marking at least one of us," Pheyal's voice floated around me, and I didn't know if he was to my right or left anymore.

"Do you think it will work on a human?" Vaquel asked.

"It has to," Broma said before groaning like he was feeling exactly what I was feeling.

"I can't see." I panted and rubbed my hands over my arms, feeling them tingle under the touch.

"Do not panic." Broma's voice felt far off, and yet so close, like I could reach out and grab him.

"That's exactly what someone would say when there is reason to panic," I grumbled, but it wasn't panic I felt. My body felt alive with nerves firing off with anticipation for something. My pussy clenched, and I knew what my body wanted.

"The gen of finding ends when you mark us."

"How do I do that?" I didn't have fangs to bite them. And my nails were much too soft to scratch them. Bode had told me as much with unGor mates that they claimed mates with biting and scratching, marking their flesh. My nails were more likely to break than to mark them.

"Your hand was given an enzyme that will react with an oil we placed on our neck. We've each chosen a design fitting what we wish to be for you."

"Support," Vaquel promised.

"Strength," Pheyal added next.

"Everything," Broma whispered hopefully.

I chuckled. "What does everything look like?"

"The life flower of AsunGor's mountain peaks. Strong enough to withstand the greatest winds, valued more than my own life, and the rarest of blooms capable of miracles."

"On AsunGor," Pheyal added, "the life flower represents the goddess, and an agreement to dedicate everything a warrior is in service to the goddess's happiness. In service to your happiness."

"My support is for her happiness too," Vaquel defended his own mark.

I smiled, and reached out, my hand gripping through warm ormete strands until my wrist came into contact with something that tingled like my arm waking up from poor blood circulation. The ormete wrapped around me to keep my wrist in place, and I heard Broma moan. Then he lifted my hand. His tongue licked my warm wrist, and the contact made me shiver all the way down to my toes.

"What was that?"

"Our bond," he said, and my vision cleared to see the strange, and beautiful flower etched into his neck. The same tattoo was on my wrist. "That one is so everyone can see it. The next one will be just for us."

"The next one?"

Broma smiled at me and kissed his way from my wrist up to my elbow and inhaled my scent.

"You promised that spot was mine," Pheyal growled territorially.

"You can discuss that with our mate later," he licked my inner elbow, and I groaned. I felt hands lifting my shirt over my head, but they weren't Broma's as he was kissing my stomach, inching my pants down. His ormete were caressing my skin as his mouth suckled at the sensitive skin at my hip, leading between my legs.

"I've got her," Pheyal assured, his firm chest was now behind me as he nuzzled into my neck.

My weight was lifted as his arms went under mine, allowing Broma to remove my pants. He tossed them at Vaquel, who lifted them to his face and inhaled the scent of my arousal.

I never thought I would be doing any of this with multiple men, but I wasn't scared, and it didn't feel as exposing as having strangers watching me. Pheyal and Vaquel were strangers, I thought oddly, but I felt safe.

"Why do I feel so safe with you?" I turned my head up to stare at Pheyal as he wrapped his arms around me. I reached up to touch his ormete, and they wrapped around my arm with a light squeeze. I watched as the ormete under his braid rubbed at my elbow.

"Because you are safe," Pheyal smiled. He shivered with a groan as my fingers gently glided across his scar under his blind eye. His ormete glowed, making his dark grey skin sparkle like stars. Then Broma's tongue flicked between my legs, and I moaned. My arms flung up behind me to wrap around Pheyal's neck for support. A tingling sensation rippled through my body, and my elbow warmed.

Broma propped my thighs on his shoulders while I felt his ormete put pressure at my entrance, teasing in little pulses as his tongue played around my clit. With a gasp, I clenched my thighs around him, and I felt warmth tingle through me again.

"What are you, a wall?" Vaquel teased Pheyal as he leaned over to gently take my chin in his hand and guide my mouth to his, whispering, "Do you want to know where I want to share our mark?"

My lip trembled as Broma worked his ormete against my sensitive flesh. I moaned with a nod, as Vaquel captured it with a kiss that was slow and deepened as I moaned again. His tongue slipped into my mouth, and he nipped at my bottom lip, tugging it gently back as his ormete rubbed against my teeth and along the inside of my lip. He pulled back and his ormete laced through my black hair, guiding me to his neck. "Mark me, little mate."

I panted as Broma increased the rhythm of his mouth. An ormete tentacle penetrated deeper into my pussy, and I clenched around him as I dove forward to bite down on Vaquel's neck to muffle my building scream. My orgasm rippled through my body and warmth tingled at my lip.

"If you marked her tongue, I will duel you, even if you are my sworn brother," Pheyal growled.

"I want to feel it every time her tongue flicks against her lip and every time her pretty mouth sucks our fingers, or our—"

He was cut off as my head swung back, resting on Pheyal's shoulder as I rocked against Broma's face.

"Yes, yes, oh fuck," I screamed with a squirm.

"That's it; feed the bond with your pleasure," Vaquel said with soothing encouragement.

Broma's tongue lapped up my cum as he groaned. He pulled back to lick his chin. Broma took his fingers and swiped up my lips to scoop up my juices. Bringing his fingers to my lips, I smelled myself on him. Was this what it felt like to feel no shame? To be truly accepted?

I liked it, and I wanted more.

Chapter Sixteen
Broma

Evie's hips rocked against me, wanting more from me even after retrieving her juice for the gen finding ceremony. All she had to do was gift the taste to Pheyal and Vaquel to accept them into her delegation, but I could not initiate it.

It was her decision.

"What will you have me do with this offering?" I watched her as she guided my fingers to her mouth and for a moment, my heart sunk for Pheyal and Vaquel. She would not give it to them, but that did not mean they wouldn't join her delegation in the future. Her silvery eyes watched me intently, and my worries for my brothers vanished as I soaked in the view of her tongue, stroking my fingers clean.

Then, as her tongue flicked the top of my fingers, she shifted her lustful eyes at Vaquel, who leaned in. He was drawn to the way she dragged her lower lip up my slick fingers. His mark glowed, and he growled as her hand gripped his ormete and pulled him towards her.

As their mouths met, and he glowed in response, I knew then that she was sharing her juices with him and he was accepted. It was surprising to see Vaquel chosen as second, and he would not live that down to tease Pheyal about it later, I thought with amusement.

Warmth filled my ormete as I watched her other hand reach up for Pheyal. He grunted to signal Vaquel to give him his space, and he sucked on Evie's lower lip where his mark rested before easing back.

"Mmm," my mate moaned as she kissed Pheyal. His ormete glowed, and my whole body vibrated with need to fill her more. It was my turn to grunt at him, to signal my growing need for our beautiful and sweet delegate.

My cock swelled to cover her in my scent. Pheyal kissed her deeply as he positioned his arms under her legs and lifted them up for her to spread for me as Vaquel turned her chin to face him again, pulling her from her kiss to allow him to taste her again.

All that mattered was her happiness, and each of us could feel that each of us played our parts in it.

As I positioned my cock at her mating seam, I paused to feel her juice drip across the tip. I rubbed myself across her to coat my mating ormete. She squirmed and bucked her hips, almost spearing herself on me before I could revel in this moment longer.

She hadn't seen my mating cock before, and I needed her to know what we were sharing together. "Look at me, mate."

She whimpered as Vaquel released her from his kiss, and her beautiful eyes fluttered open to take me in with a gasp. The mating cock throbbed at the sight of her taking me in. Ormete strands glowed and spread out to massage her thighs, wrapping around them to pull her closer. Pressing my cock at her entrance, I groaned at the sensation of her warmth and the pressure of her sheath opening for me while suctioning me in deeper as her hips lifted to meet me.

"Goddess! Evie, you're taking me so well."

She moaned and nipped at Vaquel's lip. He swallowed her mewling noises before encouraging her to take me deeper still. "Let me help you, precious mate." His hand reached down to slip between her legs, and touching my mating ormete strands. I tensed up and groaned, stilling as he rubbed gently down until his fingers pet gently at her bundle of nerves above, where I felt her clench around me. She moved against his fingers, and slowly I filled her more with each rock of her hips, supported by Pheyal's strong arms behind her. I shivered as his finger eased into her entrance, gliding against my cock.

Then her sweet voice filled my ears as Vaquel rotated his finger along my cock, easing her open for me. "Fuck, fuck," she panted for me. For us. "Don't stop," she begged as she thrust her hips up, and I sunk deep as Vaquel's finger slid out. Her head swung back with a moan, and I cupped her cheek with my hand to guide her back to me.

"Perfection," I grit out, barely containing myself with the way she squeezed me so tight.

Pheyal moaned with us, and his breathing came in quick rasps as he confessed with a strained expression, "I can't hold... Unngh... My mating cock it's... I..." He panted and Evie squeaked as her pussy clenched around me more.

He was filling her and pressure built under my mating cock, tightening me within her further. I stilled, allowing him to settle before I continued the bonding ceremony.

"Good job, my mate," I whispered soothingly as I leaned over her. "Pheyal is a worthy male, who has never used his mating cock before this moment."

Guilt plagued me that I was not as worthy of a mate as he was, and Pheyal whispered huskily in her ear, but I knew his words were also meant for me, "A mating seed means nothing without you. Relax, and I will give you my strength, as I have never given another."

Her legs opened more, and I felt her muscles release to let him in.

Chapter Seventeen

Evie

Shocked and excited, I hadn't taken him fully the last time we met. His cock was a thicker tentacle with smaller glowing strands surrounding it. They wrapped around me and pulled me in until I felt the pressure building inside as he filled me. Broma kneaded my hips as my legs draped over Pheyal's arms. His hands secured me as Pheyal adjusted me down his supportive torso until I felt a new sensation tickle at my ass.

I squeaked as a small tentacle put pressure in a place I deemed an exit only. A larger tentacle hardened between my cheeks, rubbing until my skin tingled with liquid warmth. Pheyal grunted, and he rubbed the liquid against my ass, pushing it in with the smaller tentacle until two smaller tentacles tugged my ass in opposite directions. It felt surreal as it slipped in and out. More smaller tentacles were like warm small fingers working me open as his cock dripped warm liquid between my cheeks, lubricating me, and then I clenched down on Broma's cock, seated deep inside me with a moan, while Pheyal's cock pressed to join the other smaller tentacles.

I looked over to watch Vaquel rubbing his cock in his hand; smaller tenacles reached out to rub against my stomach as he stroked himself.

"I can't..." Pheyal grunted as he pressed his cock into my ass. Broma stilled atop me as I squirmed. "I've never..." he panted, whispering in my ear, "I've never felt this pull before. Please, my strength, let me fill you."

I whimpered my consent, and I opened my legs to relax them to let him in more. Pheyal didn't move his cock but let Broma guide my hips with a slow rocking motion. My clit rubbed against Broma's tentacles, and his cock hit deep, striking a sensitive spot that drove me wild. I had trouble staying slow as my limbs flailed with the sensations building up inside me.

"I need..." I gasped. "I need..."

"That's it. Almost there, aren't you? Tell us what you need," Broma demanded with a restrained grunt.

"Fuck, Oh, my fucking—" I couldn't speak as I panted and moaned, rocking until my limbs spasmed and I lost control.

Warmth swelled inside me, rippling more sensations as what felt like ropes of shooting liquid shocking me as Pheyal shuddered beneath me. His arms wrapped around me, holding me tight as he grunted. I opened my eyes to see Vaquel throw his head back and moan; his hand stilled on one last stroke of his cock as it sprayed on my stomach and up my chest. His cum glowed like silver in the starlight, and exploded over his cock, covering his own hand as it overflowed with more cum cascading with another slow stroke of his hand.

My body heated with ecstasy as Pheyal's tentacled cock softened, but stayed inside me, throbbing.

Broma feathered his fingers through my black hair and leaned in to kiss me. As his lips took mine, his hard cock pulled back and then thrust in once more. I moaned into his mouth as he worked inside me, cradling my head as Pheyal held my back against his chest.

"Don't stop," I panted, and he pumped inside me faster.

"Whatever you need," Broma promised, as he glowed above me.

In and out, he thrusted, bringing me closer to shattering again. Everything was so sensitive, I didn't think I could handle any more when his cock swelled inside me and he hit so deep I clawed at his back to feel more of him. Pheyal held me tight, and Broma kissed me, matching my hunger.

"Do you feel that, little mate?" Pheyal whispered huskily in my ear. "He holds himself for you. Will you let him fill you?"

"Yes," I whimpered against Broma's lips, begging him to make me feel full. "I'm so close." I rocked my clit against him and squeezed around his cock, sending him over the edge.

"Everything," he moaned, "For. You." His cock pulsed, and I felt the warmth of his cum fill me in waves. As Broma eased back, I felt his cum overflow, dripping down my ass, before he thrust back inside me with a heady groan that I eagerly devoured as I kissed him. My walls milked him, feeling my whole body quake with my own release. Pleasure rippled through every nerve, and I tensed up, riding the feeling until my limbs were jelly.

I sighed with contentment at the fuzzy lightness I felt as my pussy throbbed and ached from the most world-shattering sex I'd ever experienced.

Worth it, I thought as Broma gently placed my head onto Pheyal's shoulder, and I felt Broma's cock ease out of me. Despite his absence, I still felt so warm and full. Broma's hand scooped up the cum dripping slowly down my thigh to push it back inside me.

"Be careful with lifting her," Broma said to Pheyal. "It's important the bond takes with her."

"You don't have to remind me of what's at stake if it doesn't." Pheyal kissed the top of my head.

I called out, "Vaquel?"

"I'm here," he assured, and I smiled lazily. "You must stay still until the mating seed thickens."

"Hmm," I moaned, not caring what they did with me while I felt so relaxed and yummy all over.

If this was how Violet felt with Roe-el, I understood why she was so adamant that I try a warrior for myself, even if I decided to go the unGor route over the necia.

Alien mating made my body feel exquisite.

I'd be so embarrassed to admit this to Violet later. She may have been on full display with other warriors watching, but I allowed more than one warrior to play with me, even if it was a more private affair.

I yawned and Pheyal lifted me to some place soft, while Broma's fingers did a pleasant edging push at my entrance to push more of his cum back inside me. My eyes were heavy with sleep, and I moaned, liking the way Broma lazily rubbed back and forth through my swollen lips. While I rocked against his hand to let that fuzzy warmth radiate through me in delicious waves, I nuzzled into Pheyal's chest. His cum became stickier, and I shuddered with a small jolt as Broma rubbed. I felt like it vibrated through my whole stomach, making my toes curl.

"My seed has thickened enough where you can sleep without worry," Broma said, settling on my other side. He nuzzled into my neck and inhaled my scent deeply.

I giggled. "What does that even mean?" Why would I be worrying about sticky cum? So what if we made a mess? We could just clean it up later. I was too tired to clean up now. Broma's fingers wandered in lazy strokes across my breasts and down my stomach, spreading the lotion of Vaquel's seed on my skin. It should have been gross, but I just snuggled in more and smiled.

Vaquel grunted from the foot of the bed at us, and Pheyal motioned to my legs. His eyes widened and then a big grin showed off his fangs as Vaquel moved my right leg over and rested his head on my thigh as he hugged my other leg. His finger traced my thigh and then he licked it with a groan. His ormete wrapped around my thigh and kneaded into my ass.

"Thank you for choosing me," Vaquel mumbled as he kissed my leg and his ormete rubbed all over as his nose buried near my clit, making me giggle with a squirm.

"Choosing us," Pheyal corrected as he pet my hair back from my forehead.

"Keep choosing us," Broma whispered into my neck, his tongue licking up to my ear contentedly.

"Mm-hmm," I mumbled my agreement as I laced my fingers through Vaquel's ormete on my stomach before falling asleep.

Chapter Eighteen

Broma

"She's asleep," Pheyal stated happily.

"So is Vaquel," I added with my own yawn. I'd wetted my cock before, but I'd never bonded before her, and it was a completely different experience. "You were smart to wait for this," I confessed. "It's nothing like giving pleasure to another."

"It was my father who told me it is different and encouraged me to do what you have done so that I know the difference."

"But you didn't?" I asked him curiously. Now that we were part of a shared bond, I felt more comfortable asking him these things.

"I believed him, and I wished to wait until I felt the undeniable urge that a bond pulls you to complete. It was so strong of a desire to have her so full of my seed that it overflowed from her. It felt like my very heart couldn't be contained and it was my way of giving her my strength where she became the very essence of what held me together. It was as my father described and better."

"It is much better," I agreed.

"Don't leave," Vaquel mumbled as he nuzzled into our mate's legs, covering his ormete in the residue of my seed as he slept. Evie seemed to pat his head, comforting him, but her breathing was too deep to be awake.

"Will he be okay?" I wondered with concern.

"He still thinks of his blood brother, taken by slavers many stars ago..." Pheyal sighed. "It would break him to have this bond rejected after he was forced to bond with the trill and then rejected for your safety in the Blue District. Too much for someone as sensitive as him."

"Vaquel?" I chuckled at the idea of such a strong male being sensitive, but I understood what he meant by too much loss for any warrior to take. It was a terrible feeling when I felt the ache of Evie leaving for the first time. If she left again, it would be the death of me.

"He is more growl than bite," Pheyal replied with a shared rumble that made our mate groan. We both stilled, not wishing to wake her.

"In the morning, I will meet with the commander to come to an agreement that I'm sure will be acceptable after showing him my mating mark."

"I request to join you, just in case they choose to duel. I won't allow you to be harmed before completing the bonding with our mate. The first seed is to bond. The second seeding will allow her to hold our offspring. She will need to be carrying your second seed to bond permanently and for the clans to accept her, and..." he stopped himself. This was the most he'd spoken to me in one conversation.

"We are brothers," I reminded him.

He kissed the top of Evie's head and his ormete wrapped within her dark, silky hair.

"And I don't want the same rivalry you share with your own blood brother to happen to our offspring."

My mouth was suddenly dry and uncomfortable. My brother Braukan was my younger brother, second offspring of our mother, meaning I am the only offspring that any unGor knows for sure who's seed fathered me.

Pheyal added quickly in my silence, "I know it has always been done to have the first offspring be from the first bond, but I wish to add my seed to yours so our offspring will not feel pressured to fulfill a commission, or our future offspring to resent them for simply being born first. It is our legacy to make, if we wish it to be."

He was right. Braukan might not have been as dedicated to destroying me if he felt he was more equal to me. But being the first offspring, and the only offspring that anyone knew for certain was that of a great commissioner, who only lived long enough to have me before he died on a mission to Delta Fal. Commissioner Gelbrauk. I was named after his father, and because of his death, my mother named her next son Braukan to memorialize him, even though he was not his offspring.

"My father was a great male, so I'm told."

"He was. He was alive during the first trill visit. It was because of him and your mother that we established policies to work with them while maintaining our own laws. If it weren't for them, my father said we would have been nothing more than a memory, like that of the Shol. Or slaves to do their dirty work, like that of the necia."

"We will have to lie until Braukan stops campaigning against me."

"But you will not claim first offspring?"

"Our offspring is more likely to be from my seed regardless of if you add your own seed, but you know this already," I reminded him of what we were both agreeing to.

"But we can still tell all our offspring that the first born is just as likely to be from either of our seed. It should ease their struggles."

"I will support it with Evie's consent."

"Understood." Pheyal yawned, and we both silently agreed it was time to allow sleep to take us.

This was a feeling I never wanted to lose. My delegate, surrounded by those who would die to protect her and bring her happiness. I nuzzled into her neck and felt Pheyal's ormete warm against my own as we shared tangling up in her black mane. Vaquel's butt adjusted against my leg, as Evie's leg moved to drape over his shoulder. The air smelled of our bond, and I smiled.

This was everything.

Chapter Nineteen

Evie

I woke to Vaquel nuzzling his nose into my vagina, and my sides being colder than I'd like with the clear absence of Broma and Pheyal.

Vaquel's tongue flicked out and I moaned as he worked against my clit. I guess that was one way of waking up.

"What are you doing?" I giggled with a squirm.

"Mmmm, having breakfast," he mumbled and sucked in a wonderful rhythm that made me buck against him.

"I'm... ummgh... I'm..." I gasped out as his ormete plunged into my vagina with a squelching sound. Embarrassed, I tried to pull away, but his ormete were tangled with my legs.

"Goddess, I love that sound," he said before blowing through his lips to make them vibrate on my clit as his ormete made loud suctioning sounds like he was playing with putty inside my cunt.

I giggled as I moaned against him. "Why does it sound like that?"

"It's Broma's seed preparing your womb to grow our offspring. Consider it like a universal womb that is absorbing into your mating organs." Vaquel didn't stop fucking me with his ormete tentacles as he spoke between licks and kisses on my clit. "UnGor are considered a universal species, capable of breeding with anyone, male or female. Though our females are a more universal receiver, while males are capable of breeding anyone. Oh, Goddess, thinking about you swelling with our offspring is making my mating cock hard. Let me taste you," he mumbled the last part as he buried his face into my folds, devouring me.

Panting with heat building up within me, I squeezed around his ormete and shattered into his open mouth, dribbling down his chin.

Vaquel laps up my cum and then sits up to scoot to the edge of the bed, grunting.

"Yes, yes," he repeated with more groans, hunched over the side of the bed, his arm vibrated with the movement of him stroking himself. "So close." His ormete glowed as he chanted my name, "Evie, Evie... my... nngh... mate."

I sat up to wrap my arms around him and peek my head over his shoulder, startling him.

"Great... Nnnghaagh..." he moaned out, losing his grip on his cock.

"Don't stop on my account," I said, nipping at his ear. I was pretty sure he wasn't finishing inside of me because of Broma's seed doing whatever unGor seed did to promote fertility. I grew giddy at the idea of finally being pregnant after so many miscarriages. I had to ask, "If you fucked me right now, would I get pregnant?"

He began stroking himself again. "Not yet, but keep talking about it, Evie. Talk about how you want me to fill your womb with my seed. Tell me my mating cock makes your clit ache for me. Tell me..." he hitched on a moan as his strokes sped up.

I watched as his cock swelled and the ormete tentacles around it quivered, wrapping around his hand with desperate need.

My stomach heated and my heart ached as he closed his eyes, waiting for me to encourage him and whisper sweet nothings in his ear. I wanted more. I climbed off the bed, and he whimpered as the touch of my breasts left his back.

"Keep your eyes closed," I whispered, and he squeezed them shut. With a hand on each of his shoulders, he stilled, but didn't open his eyes. The bed shifted as I used him to steady myself, placing one foot on either side of his legs. Then I lowered myself down until he had to move his arm that was holding his cock.

"Evie?" he questioned, but still didn't peek.

My mind kept repeating that he was my only mate that didn't fill me with his seed. A pull within me begged to remedy that. I seated his cock at my entrance, his hands gripped my hips, but he didn't pressure me.

"I've always wanted a family," I confessed to him. Though, I never thought it would be a family of aliens, three large hunky ones with tentacle cocks at that.

He groaned as I pushed the tip of his cock in.

"Tell me it's true." I followed his lead of wishful thinking. "Tell me being full of your cum will make our family grow."

"Nephing stars," Vaquel strained out what I assumed was unGor cursing. His ormete glowed as they reached out for me as his eyes squeezed closed to remain faithful to our agreement. "I'd wish upon them all to keep you full of my seed for the rest of our lives."

"Why?" I asked him, leaning into his ear. "You hardly know me." It was true, and yet that didn't stop me from sinking down his shaft another inch.

He moaned, and I felt his cock twitch, making me wiggle to rock him in farther.

"We don't believe in fate," he gritted out, "bonds can be made with anyone, but," he quickly added, "I've bonded before, and it was nothing like this. It's like I can feel it in every fiber of my being that you are every happiness I could have asked for, and that you would have wanted me even if we'd met differently." He paused and continued, "That I would have wanted you, even if Broma told me I couldn't have you."

"Could he do that?" I asked.

"I'd have dueled for you," he said with certainty, but I remembered that none of his adornments or trophies were collected from battles or duels.

I rocked myself until the tentacles around his cock twisted together and slipped between my lips, making me gasp.

He grinned mischievously. Then he rolled them and rubbed. They slipped up and down as I rocked him in and out, hearing the squelch of Broma's thickened cum coating Vaquel's cock. I shuddered with each roll of my hips, my clit rubbing against his pulsing tentacles.

The need grew within me. "Fuck, Vaquel! I'm so full," I whined with a moan.

He held my ass as he stood from the bed and flipped us around for him to be atop me with a growl. I smiled, seeing his eyes still closed.

"Mine," he ground out as he thrust into me, taking control. I mewled with pleasure before his cum hit so deep inside I felt my whole body spasm, arching into the feeling.

With each thrust, his cock eased out a little more until he was edging my entrance, and his cum was dripping down my ass and onto my stomach.

"Now you're full, my little mate," Vaquel said with a satisfied grin as he finally opened his eyes, breathing heavy over me. He rubbed his cock along my seam, pushing his cum back inside me. "Stay still." He kept his cock pressed against me like he was keeping the warmth inside me, and I moaned, feeling everything tingle. A slow build of sensations made me shiver and his tentacles rubbed slow circles around my clit until he lifted and lightly smacked them down in a series of little taps, firing off my nerves where I squirted with my own release.

"Fuck!" I moaned, pulling at my hair.

I looked up to see Vaquel lifting a tentacle to his fingers to scoop my juices from it, mingled with his own. His tongue flicked out, and he moaned. "We taste good together."

I didn't know what came over me, but I liked every second of it. "Do we?"

He nodded and leaned down to kiss me. I tasted us on his lips, and on his tongue that played against my own.

I chuckled. "I should probably clean up now."

"Our seed will absorb," he insisted.

"Mmm, not that part, the rest of me. I like the full feeling of your cum inside me."

Vaquel inhaled the scent around me. "All of our cum is inside you. This should deter the advances of your necia mate, but if you want him, then you should make sure to have his seed mingle with ours soon, before it absorbs fully."

"You mean Wren-Kal?

Vaquel nodded with a cute pout. He didn't seem excited about sharing more than he already was.

"Seems like too much work," I confessed. "I think three mates is already a bit greedy."

"Greedy?" He pondered the word and then shook his head. "As an unGor, it would be our own greed to keep you to ourselves if another mate could bring you more happiness. I'm a rather greedy male, and while Broma and Pheyal aren't here to scold me, I'll tell you that I don't want more mates to share you with. The tactician always gets to please a mate last, and you sought me out to fill you first this rising. I wish to do it many more times."

He rubbed his cock against me, and it came away sticky, with ropes of cum webbing between us.

Like he was summoning them both, Pheyal and Broma came through the door as Vaquel was atop me.

"I should have suspected you couldn't behave," Pheyal grumbled, but it was more of a pout than being upset with us.

Broma chuckled. "Don't blame him for something neither of us would have resisted against."

"You're not upset?" I squeaked and peeked around Vaquel to see Broma lifting a brow in confusion.

"It is preferable to keep you full until the bond between us can withstand one of us being parted from you without harming our ormete. Often, a Gengaktor Ceremony will last many dan stars. We returned when we felt the pull of your desire. Will you allow me to brush your black ormete?"

I nodded, sitting up. Vaquel eagerly rolled off and lifted my feet to place them on his lap. His ormete strands played between my toes, making me giggle. "That's ticklish."

Broma climbed behind me and stroked his fingers through my hair. Pheyal sat on the side of the bed and swiped his hand across my stomach, then lifted his hand to Broma.

"What are you doing?" I asked as I watched Broma finger some of Vaquel's cum and then using it as he worked it through my hair.

"Our seed is used across the galaxy for many things besides fertility," Pheyal explained. I watched as Vaquel rubbed his sticky cock on my feet and then massaged them.

Pheyal lifted my hand gently and pet my arm—rubbing cum into my skin like lotion. Each of them tended to me with focus and affection. Broma massaged my temples, then worked his fingers down around my scalp—and then brushed through my strands. It felt so good that I didn't even care that I was being bathed in alien cum.

The more Pheyal rubbed my arms, the stickiness went away, and it felt more and more like lotion, until a section was dry, and he'd move onto the next part of my body. Vaquel started with my feet and moved up my legs. I leaned against Broma's chest, and he adjusted to play with my hair, using his ormete instead of his hands.

I was cared for, I thought with joy.

Would they leave me? My heart ached. I hardly knew them, and yet the idea of not having them hurt so deep. They were all so gentle with me.

"I'm sorry," Vaquel finally said, making me open my eyes from the pampering.

I was going to ask for what, but realized he wasn't talking to me, but Broma.

"There are plenty more opportunities for Pheyal and me to bathe her in our own seed."

"She smells mostly of me," Vaquel said with a grin. He was pleased about it, but they had their own dynamic to figure out, too.

"It will change as she absorbs the rest of our seed inside her." Broma kissed the top of my head and whispered to me, "I've arranged a meeting with the commander. Would you like to join me?"

I nodded and looked around for the lav station. "I should clean up first," I said.

"If that will make you more comfortable," Broma motioned with his ormete to Pheyal to show me where the cleaning station was. Vaquel sighed, like the decision made him sad.

"Ignore him," Broma assured me while taking one more inhale of my hair before assisting me to scooch from the bed. "Our seed has been absorbed into your skin, washing will not remove it, but if you could hold your hand over your mating seam to prevent the powder from trying to clean while our seed is still within you, we would be honored at the decision."

"Oh." I hadn't thought about that. "Will I get pregnant from keeping your seed?" I wasn't sure if I was ready for that yet, even if the idea of having a family made me smile.

"No," Vaquel answered. "Our seed is preparing your fertility with us, but our seed alone won't give you offspring until the bond completes."

I walked to the lav station, feeling a delicious sensation of fullness move inside me with each step. It was like I had a dildo pushed up inside of me and it stimulated my walls as I moved. I purposefully squeezed my thighs together as I stepped to feel even more. Already, I was feeling like I was building a smaller orgasm just from walking.

All three of my mates groaned behind me like they could feel it, too.

"This is why Gengaktors do not end quickly," Vaquel stated with a growl.

"If it was an option, I would have taken our mate back to AsunGor first," Broma agreed.

"Yes, we'd stay in the commissioner's estate until the bond completed and show her all the many blessings of our home," Pheyal said with a grunt.

"Are you okay?" I asked them, rubbing my legs together again.

"Enter that lav station before we change our mind about allowing you to leave this room. I do not mind rescheduling with the commander," Broma said, moving towards me with his hand rubbing his pants.

I flushed with heat. I didn't think I could be any more full, but that didn't mean I didn't want to try.

"You know we should wait until our seed replenishes," Vaquel tried to reason, but hadn't dressed since this morning, and his cock was at attention within his hand. It was like he was squeezing it to hold himself back.

"Only yours has been spent," Pheyal grumbled. His arms were crossed over his chest as his nostrils flared. "I can make room for my seed in her if she desires."

I smiled to myself and rushed into the bathroom. The door closed behind me and I giggled like a kid sneaking candy. What the fuck was wrong with me that I was so giddy about this whole situation? They were mine, I thought as I hugged myself.

My foot pressed on the floor where the toilet came out. I squatted to pee over it, before I felt their cum slip down my thigh and I panicked. Jumping up from the toilet, I squeezed my thighs together and cupped my vagina with my hand. In that moment, I realized I didn't want to lose that full feeling and I liked knowing I was absorbing their seed. I wanted it.

I went into the lav shower and cupped myself as I peed, standing up. It smelled like har fruit, and I giggled again because it reminded me of eating asparagus on Earth, but much sweeter.

The powder fell from the ceiling, and the wind blew it around me, sticking to my skin and doing what it did—clinging to debris and grime to clean until all of the powder got sucked up into the vents. I kept my hand over myself to protect the seed within.

When I exited, I paused at the mirrored surface of the wall and stared. My skin was still sparkly and like I had a peachy glow about me. My hair was silky and smooth. My fingers glided through the strands. It was so soft and had a luxurious sheen. I felt like I'd come from a spa treatment.

"Bode?" I whispered.

"What can I assist you with?" he asked.

"You said unGor seed was popular for fertility treatments?"

"Yes, unGor seed is a popular trade commodity and used often for fertility."

"Just fertility?"

"Other uses for unGor seed, commonly referred to as kengak are: lotion for trill with oil gland blockages, beauty treatments for skin and hair, as well as many other unconventional uses both topically and ingested. It is a costly resource, and used primarily by wealthy species, or those with outlaw connections.

Kengak is often harvested from mated males as they produce higher yields with greater user benefits."

The bracelet given to me by Mier-Lo beeped and I remembered that they had warned me of what would happen if Bode didn't behave on the ship.

"Was that you?" I squeaked.

"My apologies," he droned with no concern about my life. "It is merely a warning to not let my signal reach out beyond my portable hard drive. It senses when I access my external data stored in your spine."

"You're what? In my what?"

Broma rushed to open the lav door, and saw me standing there, heaving.

"Evie?" Vaquel asked, worried behind him. They were dressed, and Broma was wearing his official robes.

"Apparently, I have a chip in my spine," I said through a clamped jaw.

Broma offered me some clothes, but I couldn't seem to move while processing this information. Like I was a doll, he assisted me in wrapping a robe around my shoulders and then something around my waist while the flaps were open. I blinked back to reality, and watched as he kneeled before me, wrapping straps between my thighs like bondage strips.

"What are those?"

"UnGor mating harnesses."

"Plural?"

"Pheyal requested to help you with the chest harness."

"What's that?" I pointed to the thing that looked like a strap with rubber balls on it.

"This will assist in making walking easier during our mating season. Many females have an urge to hold themselves on instinct, and this will free up your hands to do other things besides worry about the loss of our seed."

He eased my hand from my crotch, and I hadn't realized I never let go since the dust shower. I guess he was right about that instinct. My hand resisted him as he slid my fingers away, and he smiled at me reassuringly.

"Would you like me to hold your hands as Vaquel secures the harness?" Broma asked.

Before I could answer, Vaquel offered his hands and took mine in them with a soft squeeze that comforted me. "I've got you." Then he nodded to Broma to finish.

He pushed the first ball on the strap, and it popped open like a suction cup. Delicately, he placed the suction on my slit, and I squirmed at how sensitive I was, but as soon as it latched, I had a sense that it was calming my overstimulation.

"How is that possible?"

"It will hold your nerves in place, so they are not brushing against things and causing you to crave us before you are ready again."

Then the next, larger ball slid across the strap as he got it into position. He pressed it at my entrance, and I moaned as it eased inside me. His finger moved the skinny strap through my ass cheeks like a thong, and then I gasped as the final smaller ball was pushed into my butt. I heard the click of the strap being fastened to the back of the strap resting at my waist.

"And I just walk around like this?"

"Yes, it should feel secure and help ease the need of mating until we can bond again."

Vaquel tugged me forward while holding my hands as if to get me to walk and test it out.

As my foot stepped forward, I felt the way the ball in my vagina rotated with me, sending a lovely thrill zinging through my body, but I didn't have any fear or urge to hold myself to keep their seed in.

"I thought it would take away the pleasure?"

"It's not meant to," Broma said while standing. "The suction will dull the nerves, but the plug serves two purposes: to keep our seed in and ease your worry, and to stimulate you just enough to prevent the buildup of your body thinking you've stopped mating too soon. Consider it like a reminder that you are safe and will mate again soon."

Pheyal held out the harness for my chest with little suctions for my nipples, and a guard flap that seemed to sit on my shoulder.

"What's that part for?"

"We will wish to use this part of your body to bite you to complete the bonding ceremony. This is to protect you from any harm to come to that skin."

Strange enough, once I was all strapped up, and covered in a robe, I did feel comfortable, and I appreciated that lovely warmth with each step I took.

Wren-Kal wasn't waiting outside our door as we left, but he was hovering in the same meeting room we'd come from the day before, along with Commander Roe-el.

"My mate cares for Girl," Roe-el spoke, and I nearly choked, remembering I still haven't corrected him on what my name was.

"Only Violet calls me girl," I interjected with a smile. "It's a term of endearment for friends, but my name is Evie."

"Evie," he corrected himself. "Violet wishes for you to join our tribe, care for our offspring, and stay by her side."

I nodded, wanting that too. We had agreed, and she must have told him about that.

Then Roe-el glared at Broma. "You have disrespected our tribe by marking claim on a female bonded with a commander's mate. I've been informed recently that her contracted mate has been respectfully developing a bond without using mating lures like you have clearly violated."

"Like you have clearly violated," Broma corrected him, alluding to the way he had claimed Violet himself.

Roe-el's voice rose as he restrained his annoyance. "This ship is under tribal law, Commissioner. You are considered on foreign soil as a diplomat with only the rights that I extend to you. Your contract is void, but ours is still very much enforceable."

"Enforceable, you say?" Broma didn't get riled up by the threat, but I felt uncomfortable with the rising tension. I rocked my hips on the chair, feeling the comfort of the ball rotating inside me from my harness. *This contraption was h*eaven sent, I thought, as I gripped the chair arm tightly, trying to stop myself from moaning.

Chief Wren-Kal growled at the wall, his fists creating indents in the metal behind him.

"She's clearly under the influence," Roe-el continued. "Humans are more sensitive to rutting; they flush at the mere mention of it. If you wish to prove your claim is stronger than Chief Wren-Kal's, then you will allow him to give her his blood and see if she ruts with him, too."

"Excuse me?" I sobered up from the pleasure tingling in my core.

"Agreed. But you will keep your word, as that is now of greater value than your contract to an unGor, and to the agreements we have with the Trillume Authority."

"Agreed?" I stood up from my chair in annoyance.

"It is settled then. Wren-Kal has been evaluated by the Medic Ul-Ro and his medication to prevent rut has already been cleared from his system, he will be ready for a Rakture by the time we reach Necias Prime, if not sooner," Roe-el said with dismissal. He ignored my annoyance, and proceeded to say, "Would you come with me, Evie? I'm sure my mate would appreciate hearing your voice as she rests."

"Rests?" Were they fucking all night? Is she only sleeping now?

I turned to glare at Broma with betrayal. "I am not a whore!" Then I stomped off and then glared at Roe-el to show me the way to Violet. I had a lot of things to talk with her about.

Broma sputtered with wide eyes. "Of course not. I had... I didn't..."

"Where's Violet?" I prompted Roe-el again, and he nodded for me to follow him, and I did. Leaving Broma in stunned shock. *He shouldn't be the one surprised or hurt*, I thought with irritation. He basically offered me up to Wren-Kal like our time together meant nothing, that he was happy to share me with whoever.

I get it, I thought with annoyance at myself. I invited this kind of attitude in when I allowed them all to have sex with me, but it felt more intimate than that. I thought... I didn't know what I thought anymore.

Chapter Twenty
Broma

"This is torture," I moaned to Pheyal and Vaquel. We all were in rough shape, having been separated from our mate for much too long. We were orbiting Necias Prime now, and still she refused to see us.

"At least we are still on the same ship as her. We are close enough that it is manageable."

"The only one managing well is that cold-hearted unGor over there!" I roared, pointing to Vaquel in annoyance. "I smell her on you. I know I do."

He even looked away at the ceiling with guilt, and I growled, ready to fight him.

"Fine! You're right! I have seen her. And you should be thanking me that I have! I've given her jars of our seed to help her with the withdrawal symptoms of not mating during the heat of a bond. You've produced enough of it as you grunt in the lavatory," he accused with sharp accuracy.

I couldn't even be angry at him if that was why he smelled of her. He was probably the reason any of us were functioning at all without rutting. None of us wanted to reject the bond in us, so we all suffered.

"Do not be so harsh with him," Pheyal strangely told Vaquel instead of me, who was being the harshest of us all.

"Why not?" Vaquel snapped. "He's the reason we aren't filling our mate with our seed and feeling her swell with happiness!"

"What do you mean?" Pheyal asked, and I was curious as well, since the only thing she said to me before she left was that she was not a human who did things with unpure motive and means. I agreed with her statement, but did not understand her anger.

Vaquel seethed while pointing at me, his fangs bared in anger. "He agreed to have her mate with someone else without her consent. He gave permission that was not his to give. So, she punishes us all, and if our bond is rejected, I will never forgive you!"

"Is this true?" Pheyal asked of me.

I wanted to immediately say these were false accusations; it was my gut instinct to do so. I would never...

Instead, I needed them to agree with that what I did was not what they were accusing me of. "Commander Roe-el had made it clear that he wouldn't recognize our claim to her, or hers to us unless she could resist mating with her contracted mate, Chief Wren-Kal. She has us; there is no need to mate with him—and if she did mate with him, then that was a choice we would have to accept as her mates, regardless. Evie has our scent; the necia warrior wouldn't be able to get past our smells to rut with her..."

"Had our scent," Pheyal said with a growl, growing more upset with me. "You may be young, Broma, but you are not stupid. Did you explain to our mate your intentions were not to take away her choice, but merely a negotiation tactic with the necia?"

I shook my head. "There was no time to discuss this in front of the commander."

"Waustenger!" Vaquel spat at me, and I felt even shittier because he was right. I was a betrayer of trust if she thought I had sent her off like a Blue District worker to mate with someone against her desires.

"You have harmed us all, but yourself and our mate the most," Pheyal said with a groan. "I've noticed the bulges in your ormete."

Vaquel's eyes grew wide, and he shook his head. "Have you been dropping eggs? Nephing stars!" He cursed at the wall and wrung his fingers through his own ormete like he would tear them out in shock. He paced the room and then threw his hands up. "Why didn't you say something?"

"I didn't want to rush things with our mate," I admitted.

"She should know," Pheyal urged.

"It's her choice," Vaquel agreed. "You already took a choice from her once; don't do it again."

I nodded and took a deep breath. "You're right." An unGor egg is a vital part of an offspring having the right nutrition, and it means she's bonded enough to be fertile.

Eating an unGor egg would prompt her body to accept offspring. It was her choice to make. It would surely complete our bond, but she may not want that any longer. At least, not with me.

"We're going now," Vaquel stated and stomped to the door. "She may still be mad at you, but I can tell she's hurting and you two need to fix this. For all of our sakes."

That's when I felt the tug on our bond that felt all too similar to when she left the first time. Vaquel dropped to his knees from the shock, and Pheyal roared in pain.

My own screams echoed in my ears.

The door was opened, and the necia guards rushed to our sides.

"What's wrong with them?" one asked with a wince.

Mier-Lo was walking casually down the hall in front of us.

"Commander?" Another guard asked, seeking guidance on what to do.

"I was on my way to tell you that the humans have left to seek the healers on the surface. Command has been returned to me. I'm here to inform you that you are no longer welcome on this ship and must return to your vessel."

"Evie..." I groaned, grabbing onto my head as if that would keep it together. "Get the shuttle prepared, Pheyal. We'll negotiate clearance to land on Necias Prime."

Mier-Lo clucked her tongue with amusement. Normally, this would be an intriguing gesture that any unGor would find attractive, but all it did was agitate me. "You might want to avoid any clearance that would require Chief Wren-Kal's approval. He was ready for a Rakture hunt last I saw of him, and he'd been having Ul-Ro put him under lockdown until a ceremony could be performed. I doubt you'll be getting any approval from him anytime soon."

She wasn't done gloating about our precarious situation when she added, "I'd have tried to make Wren-Kal my mate while he's vulnerable, but I don't like the idea of being planet bound, and he's closer to being an elder than to wanting to explore the stars. He's also got the same disease you lot seem to have. Falling for your pets."

"Pets?" Vaquel growled in anger.

I held up my hand to stop him from falling into her trap.

"Remember, Vaquel," I explained through the pain pulsing through my ormete the farther our mate got from us, "Necia warriors find dueling an attractive foreplay and I doubt our mate would appreciate you mating outside the delegation."

Mier-Lo smirked. "You're no fun, Commissioner Broma. You're lucky, as a Commander of a Galactic Authority vessel, I'm required to give diplomatic waiver to you on denying my rights as a tribal leader. I'll even be polite and offer you some advice. Your human will not leave the other human's side, and after Roe-el's disaster of a mating ceremony, the red-headed one has not woken."

"She's not awake?" I wondered out loud. "Is that typical for a necia mating?"

"Any warrior would have woken already, but it is normal to sleep after mating," she confirmed. "It's better for all of us if the human doesn't wake at all, but I've heard the unGor have a salve that can speed up recovery of fertility issues. I may not like the human, but what's inside her is part of my tribe, and you three can help the future warrior."

"Are you saying you'll approve our shuttle to land on Necias Prime?" I asked her.

"Go take them to the shuttle already," she commanded the necia guards next to us. "Bunch of lost souls, the lot of you. They even smell like humans, even after all this time." Mier-Lo scoffed and handed me a strange leather adornment with a red bead at the end.

"What's that?" Vaquel asked.

"It appears to be an offering," I said while lifting my brow ridge in confusion. "Is this for me?" If it was, I couldn't accept it. Whose blood was in the bead?

"I have no intentions of living on unGor," she dismissed my concern. "This is a gift for the human. A token of my acceptance of her joining the tribe. Give this to her, and you have my approval. UnGors keep their words."

"Understood. We accept."

I took the trinket and handed it to Vaquel. He would know better how to scan it and make sure it was safe to give to the human, Violet.

Chapter Twenty-One

Evie

"I'll murder you if she doesn't wake up, you know this, right?" I grumbled at Roe-el, who was rubbing her belly so much, I wondered if it would go raw. I thought about putting some of the lotion Vaquel gave me to help soothe her skin, but it felt awkward, considering I knew what it was made of now.

Rubbing my mate's cum on her stomach seemed like a bit much when she wasn't awake to agree to it.

I glared at Roe-el because he deserved it, but also, I was abnormally grumpy from withdrawals of the mate bond with not one, but three unGor mates. Ul-Ro was kind enough to come to the surface to help me and look after Violet.

"I would accept this punishment gladly," Roe-el said with distress as he watched her. He really did care about her. I could see it in his eyes, and the tender way he fussed over her for weeks.

She still wouldn't wake up, but I watched as he bled himself and tipped her head to feed her from his blood. Apparently, that was what was keeping her alive this whole time. Necia blood promoted natural healing and gave her nutrients. Or so Medic Ul-Ro said.

She was still seemingly healthy outside of being unconscious, so there wasn't much I could say against it.

"She'll be happy," I told him, "When she wakes up. She'll be happy that you're both having a baby."

"If she does not wake, I would rather rip that offspring from her womb to bring her back," he grumbled.

Medic Ul-Ro interjected, "That isn't necessary. They are both healthy at the moment."

"But she is not awake!" Roe-el roared.

"I'm monitoring the situation," Ul-Ro assured. "The scans show that she is taking to your DNA very well, just very slowly.

I've seen new tooth growth in her gums, and an accelerated healing rate."

"And her hair?" I questioned as I tugged a chunk of red hair that fell from her scalp.

"Regrowing, stronger. New follicles are forming under the scalp surface. I'm projecting that once it's finished, new hair will grow quite fast, and her new teeth are likely to be similar to ours. It is necessary to have fangs to feed our offspring."

"I could do that for her." Roe-el objected to waiting for all these changes. "She doesn't need them."

I agreed.

"Yes, well..." Ul-Ro cleared his throat and turned his attention to me. "If you could join me in the other room for a moment, Evie?"

I hesitated, but he insisted, "Commander Roe-el won't let anything happen to her."

I glared at him, because that was obviously the wrong thing to say. He'd already done something to her. But I followed him anyway.

"Has the new harness been working for you well?"

My cheeks turned rosy with embarrassment, but he was a medical professional, so I swallowed that down and nodded. "It's," I cleared my throat, "helping."

My body has absorbed everything, and Ul-Ro explained that I've become very fertile because of the effects of the kengak, a fancy term for unGor seed. Fertility by alien seed is common to cause rutting in most species, and humans were no exception, according to him. And according to my own body, I grumbled.

My body kept making me feel so empty, and when the kengak absorbed, the usual harness wasn't enough.

"Do you need a larger stimulator? Or would you like for me to initiate a low dosage of rut inhibitor?"

I shook my head. "You said that it's likely the root you would give me would do more than end my mating urges..."

Ul-Ro nodded. "It would likely counteract the kengak's effects, including your fertility. But that isn't why I asked to speak with you privately."

"Why then?"

"Chief Wren-Kal has been asking to speak with you. He has made an offering of his blood to adorn your hair, as is a common mating practice for us necia. You are not obligated to receive the offering, but I should tell you he is an honorable male and even in rut, he would wish for you to yearn for him. He refuses to leave his hut, and has made me dose him with elder root beyond its effectiveness to stop a rut, but more knock him out until it's over. He only wishes to be woken if you accept his mating offer."

He was kind to me on the ship, had cared about whether I ate, and if I was comfortable, I thought with worry.

"But he'll be okay once he wakes, right?"

"He is not the first warrior to rut," Ul-Ro assured me with a smile. "You should know, though, that a warrior like him didn't have to go into rut at all. On low doses of the elder root regularly, a warrior can avoid rut altogether, but he went off his regular dosage when he agreed to the mating contract. As he wanted to have a true mate, not just a contracted mate."

"All of that sounds like he is a good man, and I'm sure he'd treat me well..."

"But, you know necia are territorial, and seen through Commander Roe-el that Chief Wren-Kal would likely not accept other mates."

I smiled at Ul-Ro. "You're a very wise medic."

He sighed. "Wise enough to know you humans cannot be swayed by displays of strength or merit of tribal honor. I'm uncertain exactly what your mating conditions are, but I hope to understand them better so I will not be passed up the next time I meet another human."

I laughed. "Why are you so set on mating a human?"

"Queen Riley fell for our king when she thought he was nothing more than a criminal with no honor. Violet fell for Roe-el even knowing his status as commander was just a title with no ship to command. The ship was always Mier-Lo's, and he only had command because of his escort mission under the contract signed by the princess and future ruler of Trillume. He has no tribe to give her, but she still chose him over that of a commissioner for an entire planet. If humans can mate for warriors in those conditions, then I have a chance to be more than a medic for the rest of my life."

"I'm sure there are others who would see your worth beyond your title in the tribe."

He shook his head. "I would lose a Rakturan duel, and our females require winning a duel against them to be worthy of mating. I may live my whole life serving the tribe to earn privileges to bathe them, but nothing more."

I frowned.

"Evie!" I heard my name called out in desperation. I turned to find Riley rushing through the hut flap of the medical huts connected together.

"Why are you running?" I asked her, quickly meeting her halfway. She huffed and adjusted the spear at her back. She carried that thing everywhere.

"I didn't know... I'm so sorry," she said, panting.

"Didn't know what?"

"The unGor have been requesting to see you for weeks. They've been surface side this whole time. They are very sick but refusing medical treatment."

"What do you mean, they're sick?" I felt my chest clench like my heart would explode.

Her lip wobbled, and she looked about to cry, but then she angrily shouted, "Direl thought he was doing what was best for his tribe brother, Wren-Kal! He's been sneaking off in the middle of the night and I caught him doing it again this morning! He's going to regret it!"

"They're here? Are they okay?" I tried to get her to speed up and get to the point. Where were they, and are they okay?

"I'm sorry, I know you've been hoping they would come and explain themselves. My mate was trying to do something he thought would make me happy. He stupidly thought that if you mated with Wren-Kal that you would join the tribe and both me and Wren-Kal would be happy. And of course, in his mind, he knows both of us would bring you happiness, so he didn't understand. I know you've missed the unGor, and if it weren't for Violet... you would have looked for them."

"They agreed to have me fuck someone else to prove their bond was stronger..." I grumbled with my arms crossed over my chest. The panic on Riley's face reminded me that now was not the time to worry about the past. "How bad is it?"

"I didn't check..." Riley admitted sheepishly. "I just took Direl's word for it and came to get you. They said they were willing to die on Necias Prime and create a diplomatic nightmare for our tribe if they didn't get to at least talk to you. Direl was going to wait until you completed a Rakturan with Wren-Kal before telling you anything."

"Take me to them."

When I arrived at the cave guarded by several necia warriors, I realized that it was more than just Direl that had kept the unGor a secret from us.

Riley smashed the bottom of her spear into the ground with annoyance. "You are dismissed."

"Yes, my queen."

Another warrior averted his eyes, and the other bowed his head with reverence before saying, "We will submit ourselves to whatever will quell your anger. King Direl has said the unGor will gift the tribe with kengak to promote your fertility."

"Did he now? So he's making baby plans without me, too?"

"Never," the warrior denied. "It was to be presented to you as an offering."

I whispered into Riley's ear, "You know what kengak is, right?"

"We talked about it," she said with a blush. "Direl said it could help us with having an offspring of our own if I'm concerned about not being able to carry a hybrid species."

I wouldn't embarrass her with what it was in front of her tribe. She could decide about it later.

"Can I go in?" I asked her instead.

"Of course you can," she said while glaring at the warriors to not interfere.

They watched as I rushed past them to find Broma, Pheyal, and Vaquel sweating profusely in beds with a healer rubbing herbs on them.

"What's wrong with them?" I asked her.

"Evie?" Broma croaked, but when he opened his eyes, they were all milky and glassy, like he couldn't see. "I'm sorry. I didn't mean it. Forgive me."

Vaquel muttered out, "Don't mate with the necia. Remember, I'm too greedy to share you."

I chuckled with a sob of emotion because technically he was sharing me with Pheyal and Broma, but apparently, they didn't count in that statement. That was so like Vaquel. I missed being with him on the ship when he snuck out to meet me at the observatory. He kept his word about not telling Broma or Pheyal about our little meet ups; not once was I ambushed by one of them in place of Vaquel. He really did anything for me, even keeping me to himself.

Pheyal spoke next, "Do not reject us, little mate."

"Reject you?" I shook my head in denial.

"If this was rejection, then we'd have smelled like rot a while ago," Vaquel objected.

"He's right," Broma agreed. "This is my fault. Evie, please reject me alone. Pheyal and Vaquel are worthy of your bond."

My lip trembled. "What are you talking about?"

"I have not proved myself worthy," Broma said, shifting on the bed with difficulty.

"Tell her," Vaquel pressed.

"I've saved an egg for you. It will help you carry offspring so your womb will not reject a hybrid species. It needn't be with me that you use this, but it is yours to do with as you wish."

"It is why he's endured so long, keeping it safe," Pheyal stated. "Eggs do not last long outside of the ormete, and he's agreed with the terms of the necia king to leave once he knows you're where you wish to be. With or without us."

I asked Riley, "Is that true? Do I have to leave?"

Broma looked the worst of the bunch, and he lifted up a swollen ormete hiding under his braid of adornments. I reached out to him and gathered the pale tentacle in my hands gently. It glowed and peeled apart like a fruit to reveal a worm that I assumed was the "egg"?

It wiggled in my hand, and I should have been disgusted. I disliked worms, and never once touched something so slimy on Earth.

"Thank you," I said and then bent over to kiss him. Color returned to his lips when I did. His skin was still grey, but at least it didn't appear so ashen.

Riley added quietly, "I'm not sure how to help them, but I won't let anyone force you to leave—or them... if that's what you want. We could try giving them necia blood—it speeds up recovery from most injuries."

"This isn't an injury," Broma explained.

I understood now what has been happening to them. "This is because of me," I stated.

"No," he denied.

"I was angry with you, but I never wanted this and then with Violet... I didn't think..." my eyes welled up as I stroked my fingers through his ormete. My tears dripped onto his face, and I watched as color returned to his eyes. Could he see me?

Vaquel called out, "She's bonded!"

"Don't tease me, Vaquel." Broma turned away from me with distress.

"Her ormete are moving!" Vaquel continued.

Pheyal turned over with a grunt, and his eyes widened. "He is not teasing you."

Riley spoke up this time, "Evie, your hair is glowing!"

I watched as my hair reached out to tangle up with Broma's ormete.

"How is this possible?" I asked with wonder and scooped Broma's face into my hands to kiss him harder.

The egg squirmed to wrap around my wrist, and I didn't even care that it was a strange alien worm attaching to me. It was from my mate, and the more I accepted that I had never given up our bond, the more Broma's skin seemed to respond to mine.

"Don't ever try to give me away to anyone else again," I chided, and then kissed him once more.

"If all you took was me as a mate, that would be enough," he groaned out. "All I need is you."

"Hey!" Vaquel grumbled. "I could say the same about you! It's my scent on her skin." And he was right. I had been using his kengak to help ease the symptoms of my need for all of them.

I smiled and let him know that this wasn't a rejection of any of them. "I want you too, Vaquel, and Pheyal. And you," I said directly to Broma as I stroked his face.

"Just give us some time around you and we'll be well enough to repair the bond," Pheyal said from his bed, trying to lift himself up, but still so weak.

"How do I keep you?" I whispered to Broma. He was unable to move much. How do I fix this?

The deep voice of King Direl spoke from the cave's entrance, "Allowing them to taste your blood is a good start to keeping your bond strong."

"Isn't that just for necia?" Riley asked her mate.

"The unGor don't need it, but it is a quick way for their bodies to know that she has kept her bond strong even if she wasn't physically present with them. Plus, they display mating marks similar to ours after bonding. It should pep them up to finish what they must. Come with me, Pulsunne; I have some bonding planned for us as well."

Riley looked between me and my mates, and then she made a little "oh" sound before scurrying off with her mate.

I lowered my neck to Broma, and his fangs gently sunk in. Just a surface level cut to taste my blood on his tongue with a moan.

"It's true," he said with wonder and pride. "You never left us."

"If you did not break the bond, then how have you dealt with the pull of the mating heat?" Pheyal asked.

The blush on my cheeks seemed to translate to the glow in my hair and I felt like a glowbug. I guess they were going to find out anyway, I thought, and they wouldn't judge me for it.

I cleared my throat, "I've been using the harness with a bit of modifications, and Vaquel's kengak."

"I wasn't giving you just mine," Vaquel confessed. "The last one had all of ours."

"That makes sense," I said, having my own confession to make. "I tried both the jars I still had, and the last one you gave me helped my urges the most."

"She wants us all," Pheyal said with a strained huff as he forced himself to sit up and throw his legs off the side to try to come to me.

Broma kissed my neck. "Go to them before they hurt themselves to get to you. I'll figure out what kind of modifications you've made to the mating harness shortly."

I smiled and shivered with anticipation. "I'll hold you to it." I kissed his forehead, and my hair detangled from his ormete.

"Pheyal," I called out as I rushed to him next. "Don't push yourself." His fangs were already out, and my hair reached out to guide him to my neck. The bite was gentle, and all I felt was warmth when he finally licked it. I took a moment to gaze at his face and brush against the scar that blinded him in one eye. Smiling, I kissed his nose. "Thank you for not rejecting our bond."

They all could have accepted that I'd rejected them, and they would have been fine right now. They held out, knowing I'd return to them, but they had to endure the pain of the bond not being finished. And here I had thought only I was suffering from being apart from them. I was agitated because my body was on fire to be filled, and here they were literally wasting away. It meant more to me than I could ever express. They stayed for me. They chose me, even if it was easier to leave or choose someone else.

"I've waited a long time for you, little mate," Pheyal said and gave me a squeeze before motioning me to the last bed with Vaquel turned away, so he wasn't even watching us. He always felt he was going to be ignored, last to everything, and less than Broma or Pheyal.

I leaned over his face and let my hair tangle up with his ormete before kissing his cheek. "I put your seed on our mark and lick it to go to sleep at night," I whispered in his ear.

"Nephing Goddess, you know exactly what gets me hard for you," he grumbled, but I knew he was smiling. He rolled over to grab me to sink his fangs into me. Not quite as soft as my other mates as he nipped and licked, marking me twice as many times. "Mine," he licked up to my ear and moaned.

I loved what every one of my mates gave to me, but I had a soft spot for the aggressiveness of Vaquel. He spun me around, and held me by the shoulders, kissing the markings on my neck as he said, "Stay still as our Commissioner inspects your harness. I want to see what's been keeping you from coming to me sooner."

I shivered, and he unclasped my robes to expose me to Broma, who was walking slowly towards us. He was already looking healthier. His dark grey skin sparkled like stars.

Rubbing my thighs together made the harness insert twist, and I moaned, wanting them to see what I've been hiding between my legs.

Broma kneeled before me, unbuckling the straps with a deliberate ease that was torturous to wait for. First, he released the first suctioned attachment, and immediately the air on my clit made me tingle and beg for a touch, but he denied me as he eased the plug from my ass, and the strap dangled, hanging only from the last attachment.

"Nothing unusual about those," Pheyal remarked.

With two fingers, Broma slipped them on either side of the insert, rubbing between my lips, and I moaned as he tugged, but it didn't pop out.

"Evie," Broma said my name, and I squirmed. "A normal harness would have slipped out with a simple pull."

"What are you hiding in your mating seam?" Vaquel nipped at my ear, and I leaned into his hold.

"Why don't you find out?" I nipped back and caught his lip, bringing him into a deep kiss. Moaning into his mouth, I felt Broma pull the replica of an unGor cock from my aching core.

"It isn't to size," Pheyal admonished, and I laughed.

"Prove it," I challenged him. Pheyal liked a contest, even if it was one that was easily won. He was the largest of the three of them.

Pheyal growled and Broma licked my juices from the temporary unGor cock that had held me together in their absence.

"For one, little mate, this toy doesn't have any ormete," Pheyal said, and I watched as his already hard cock got wrapped up with ormete tentacles, expanding its size. The tips wiggled at the base as they wrapped to the top and back again.

Broma tossed the toy to the side and inhaled my scent before leaning in to lick up my thigh. He gave extra attention to the mark he had given me there of the AsunGor life flower and then moaned. "You're dripping for us. And I've been especially thirsty for you."

His tongue licked between my lips to play with my clit. No longer being held back by the mating harness, I felt everything and the need to be full again drove me crazy.

Vaquel's fingers traveled down my chest and over my nipple with a flick before he swiped between my legs for his own taste. "Do you know why I'll wait for you?" He whispered as I heard his lips smack with each pop of his fingers, sucking off my juices. I whimpered and shook my head for him to tell me. "Because this isn't sharing. I'm not being nice. When they're done filling you with their seed, it will be my cock that makes it gush from your mating seam to make room for my own. I'll pump you so hard that all that's left is me. Nod if you understand," Vaquel demanded.

Pheyal chuckled and used his knuckle to turn my chin towards him. "Being away from you has made him needy. I'll make sure you're ready for him."

Broma spread my legs and then kissed my thigh before he moved out of the way to watch. "Such a pretty view." He stroked himself slowly. "Be a good girl and let Vaquel hold you up for Pheyal."

Vaquel lowered himself, pressing kisses to my back as he linked his arms under my knees. "Lean into me," he guided as he lifted me up, spreading my legs wide for Pheyal.

"Let me remind you what real unGor feels like," he said as he pressed his cock at my entrance. Needy for him, I bucked, and Vaquel backed up with a tsk of his tongue clucking to the roof of his mouth.

"Let me help you," Vaquel insisted and then eased me forward again. Pheyal gripped my hips and grunted as precum dribbled from his cock. He rubbed himself along my sensitive lips and then notched himself to edge me to insanity with dipping in and out of my pussy.

"Fuck," I swore as he did it again. My head swung back as I arched into Vaquel's support, and my arms wrapped around Pheyal's neck to pull him closer.

"Do you feel that?" Vaquel panted in my ear behind me. "How his cock struggles to fit with his ormete wrapped around it? Take your small fingers and go down there to open yourself for him."

I whimpered my agreement, and rubbed my fingers along his ormete, trying to help push it inside of me. He moved in a little bit more and we both moaned, but it wasn't enough.

"Don't you remember how I helped you before?" Vaquel urged. And I did, vividly. He used his own finger to push inside of me around Broma's cock and helped him slip inside while his finger was pushed out.

"Mmm Hmm," I agreed and rubbed my finger against my clit until I used two fingers to slide on either side of his cock and pushed until they were inside me before I rocked my pussy closer while pulling them back out.

"Nnngh, yes!" I screamed as he filled me.

"So tight," Pheyal gasped. "You take all of me so well." He gripped my hips and pulled me closer until I felt him so deep, my body spasmed.

"That's it," Vaquel cooed. "I've got you."

"Use the wall for support," Pheyal prompted Vaquel, and he scoffed in response.

"Do not make me wait longer than I must."

"Don't rush him, Vaquel," Broma said with a grunt, his cock in his hand as his ormete tentacles wrapped up his arm.

I smiled at them, loving the way they bickered together in a way that held so much warmth and understanding between them.

"Strength, support, and everything," I mumbled to myself, but I knew they heard me.

Pheyal pitched forward and worked himself inside me, slow and deep, grunting with each thrust. "I got one of my first scars from dueling the father of a female I'd refused to give my mating cock to. Word spread of how difficult I was to mate with, and my scars grew as their egos were crushed for not winning the contest that was claiming me."

"Pheyal," I moaned his name as he pumped into me, each thrust deliberate as he told me his story. He chose me to claim this victory.

Vaquel added behind me as I pulled Pheyal's lips to mine to kiss him, "He lost his eye not just to free unGor from slave trade, but because he had to kill the slaver or mate with a slave for entertainment. He saved himself for you."

Pheyal kissed me tenderly before I felt him increase his tempo. My walls squeezed around him, feeling my pleasure mount until I gripped his back and my scream muffled into his mouth. My muscles clenched and the feeling of his seed bursting inside of me undoing the last string holding me together. I collapsed into Vaquel's and Pheyal's hold.

As Pheyal eased out of me, Vaquel said, "Not so fast." His hand quickly cupped between my legs and pushed his fingers at my entrance. "I want to make sure you feel how full we make you."

Pheyal kissed me deeply, and I groaned, "Don't leave."

"I'm not going anywhere," he promised.

Broma glowed as he took over kissing me. "I should be jealous," he said between suckling on my lip and nipping at me. "But all I feel is happiness at the way you shine for us. Do you see how relaxed Pheyal is as he walks away to watch us? He can do that now without pain. What you shared with him just now made him fully bonded."

"But you were just..."

"Watching you get mated without touching you?" Broma finished for me. "I fully mated you the moment I bit you and felt that you had already accepted my bond. There is no turning back now. Do you regret it? Saying yes to me?" Broma asked as he kissed down my neck to lick the mark he had given me.

"No," I gasped and then forced myself to admit out loud what I knew long before then but couldn't say before now, "I never wanted to leave you from the moment I met you."

"Evie..." Broma stilled at my nipple, taking it into his mouth, making me whimper.

His ormete tentacles wrapped around my thighs, and a few massaged against my clit as his cock pushed into me.

"Yes," I rasped.

"You make me believe in fate," he whispered as he sunk into me and froze buried deep within me. He captured my mouth and, in that moment, I felt the world stop. I couldn't imagine how things could be any better with Pheyal's seed warming me, Vaquel's arms around me as Broma's cock thrusted to make my toes curl.

Vaquel licked my ear and said, "Are you ready to tell me how full we make you?"

Broma eased us down to the ground with me on top. That's when I felt Vaquel behind me sliding his cock and his ormete tentacles down my back and between my cheeks. I thought he was going to prepare me for what Pheyal had done last time, but he slipped past and began pushing against my entrance, where Broma already was.

"Combine your ormete and rub against her clit," Vaquel told Broma. "She likes that."

"Vaquel?" I moaned as I understood why he said Pheyal and his cock being wrapped up with his ormete was to prepare me for him.

Vaquel's tentacles prodded on all sides to ease me open more and then slipping his cock in farther until he used his ormete to wrap around my waist and guide our movements while Broma laid there with a smile toying with my clit.

"I will never tire of this view," Broma said seriously before stroking the little worm that had wrapped around my wrist lovingly. "I'll make more for you and we can make you full with our seed. When you eat this, it will attach to your womb and provide support to carry unGor offspring."

I wrinkled my nose, even though the sentiment was sweet and made me excited. "For humans, it reminds us of a worm, not an egg. Or really like a parasite is what you're describing."

"Hmm," Broma thought about this as he moaned. Vaquel's cock adjusted a little more, and I gasped.

"Relax, and let me take care of you," Vaquel soothed. "And the egg is not a parasite; it dissolves into the nutrients you need to grow life. Our family. Now, feel the way you stretch for me. Tell me how full you feel and how you crave my seed."

"Let me feel your pleasure," Broma encouraged, as Vaquel's cock slowly rocked within me.

"Do you feel how my cock makes Broma harder? How his seed squirts for us each time I thrust?"

"You talk too much," Broma grunted, but he didn't deny it, and I felt the pleasurable shock of Broma's cock hitting deeper as Vaquel eased in and out of me. I squirmed atop him and felt my body spasm so much I thought I'd push Vaquel off with my flailing, but he held me in place.

"Almost there," Vaquel whispered. "I can feel the way you squeeze us."

"It feels so good," I panted.

"So deep," Broma grunted with pleasure. His fangs bit into his own lip as he strained.

"I beg you," I moaned. They both knew what I needed. I needed to feel their seed moving inside me. I needed more. I needed all of them.

Broma shuddered beneath me, sending me over the edge I'd been waiting for. I could feel the way his seed shot out and his cock spasmed inside of me with each wave. I collapsed forward onto his chest and panted as my body quaked with my own release, and I rocked my clit against his ormete.

Vaquel lifted me from Broma's cock to speed up his thrusts as my ass lifted in the air for him. The sound of him slapping against my ass as he pounded into me made my moans echo louder.

"Fuck. You. Feel. So. Good." I screamed out as I nuzzled my face into Broma's chest. I felt the warmth of my hair tangling up with Broma's ormete, and he wrapped his arms around me.

"I hope you're not tired, little mate," Pheyal said as he kneeled to pet my hair.

Vaquel gripped my hips and thrust so deep my eyes rolled back, my toes curled, and my hand flung out to grip Pheyal's arm for support.

I fucking loved the sound of his cock slick with Pheyal and Broma's seed slapping inside of me, pushing the seed deeper, making room for his own.

"Tell me what you want," Vaquel demanded.

"I want to be so full you force the seed to drip from my pussy. Then I want you to fuck me to force it back where I need it."

"Nephing stars, you're so perfect," Vaquel moaned as he came hard, and I squirted on Broma beneath me. My body tensed up and spasmed, riding the wave until my limbs were jelly.

I squirmed and rubbed my clit on Broma, and he chuckled. "You'll feel better once you've absorbed our seed, but we'll scratch that itch for you until it's settled. A mated unGor can still pleasure their mate while they wait for their seed to replenish. Our cocks are still hard for you."

Vaquel slowly worked his cock inside of me, making me moan. I wasn't ready to be done, and I reached for Pheyal's cock. His ormete tentacles surrounding it wrapped around my hand, and I guided him to my mouth. I stuck my tongue out and licked him from base to tip, tasting both his seed and my own juices. He smelled like me, and I loved it.

"You're everything, and mine," I told them before I let the mating heat take me once more.

Chapter Twenty-Two

Broma

With our mating bond completed, I no longer felt the pain of our separation because I knew and felt the bond, no matter where she was. *I also knew exactly when Vaquel couldn't keep his hands off her and made my cock swell in public*, I thought with a playful chuckle.

Evie had decided she wanted to give the unGor egg to Violet when she understood that it didn't contain any of my genetics, like my seed. She had held off before when she thought she'd be sharing something that was only meant for her, but I would make more for her and they were hers to decide what to do with. She called the egg a worm, which I still couldn't understand.

I had looked up what an Earth worm was, and I still didn't think they were similar. An unGor egg transferred nutrients, created from my own body, and assisted the creation of life. A worm ate dirt from their planet's surface, and even had its own reproductive system, and some of them were parasites that stole nutrients from their host. If anything, her worm was more like the waustenger, but with no teeth. I'd debate this issue with her another time.

Luckily, or perhaps it was fated, the unGor egg was exactly what Violet needed to be well enough to wake from her mating slumber. Her body was struggling to provide for the life growing inside her and she didn't have enough energy left over to be awake. Her body knew that all its resources were diverted to the offspring. With the unGor egg, she awoke the very next day, and the offspring was growing much healthier and stronger without taxing Violet's body too much.

It was refreshing to see Evie happy and doing what she called "hanging" with the girls.

Not once did I see any of them "hang", but I'm told it isn't literal.

"You're certain?" I asked Medic Ul-Ro.

"Mier-Lo took the ship before I was scheduled to re-board. Honestly, I'm uncertain when she actually took off. It could have been dan stars ago if she left as soon as we landed."

"And King of the House of Nel, he knows this?" I questioned.

"He does, but he can't go himself when his death, or his mates, would put necia warriors across the galaxy in danger. If the trill wanted to take leadership again, all they'd have to do is kill them. Our independence from their control is too early to risk for one warrior."

"One warrior that tried to kill two humans," I corrected him. This set a dangerous precedent that I could not allow to stand. The trinket she gave us contained a microchip that activated the bracelets that both Violet and Evie wore from the ship to prevent any breach from AI programs.

The only reason I was talking reasonably at all right now was because Chief Wren-Kal had removed the bracelets before Mier-Lo's gift ever accomplished its goal. If he hadn't done that... both humans might have been dead right now. I say might have, because being on Necias Prime was the perfect place to be when trying to heal unknown nanotech. Their blood could have helped fight off the invasion of their systems until we could figure out how to stop it or reprogram them. I had to remind myself that even if Mier-Lo's plan had worked that Evie would still be here. That she wouldn't have been gone.

Otherwise, I would be living up to my name of being the Mad King of AsunGor.

"Vaquel would remind us to tell Evie about this," Pheyal added. I could already tell just by glancing at him that he was planning his own actions to bring Mier-Lo to his own kind of justice.

"Yes, you're right," I agreed. "But I'm told humans prefer not to know until they are certain there are no complications. Even BOD has stated Evie's desire not to be told of details that would be considered upsetting."

"Why does she choose to keep him when he implanted a chip of his hard drive in her spine without permission?" Medic Ul-Ro questioned.

"She enjoys his company, and BOD likes that she asks him questions while he is not so secretly recording her life like a human research project. She likes that she'll be useful to future humans in the universe with BOD's efforts," I told them both. Pheyal nodded, understanding that he wasn't much of a talker, like Vaquel, and there were many conversations that he didn't get to have with our mate because of that. He still liked to listen to everything, even if it is relayed by me or Vaquel.

"BOD has also generously been paying my mate ridiculous sums of credits to compensate for what he realized was a violation of her consent. She wants to use them to help fund more efforts to Earth women, so they aren't forced to choose contracts to survive, but choose contracts because they wish to," I continued, avoiding the conversation I was supposed to be having. "Perhaps we'll send a representative to Earth to encourage more mating contracts. Evie has said we should create a consulate and even get volunteer unGors to settle on Earth."

"But their air is toxic, and their cities are above the surface..." Medic Ul-Ro pointed out. Necia warriors would not survive long on Earth. Their lifespans would be reduced drastically by the toxicity levels of the air. *Humans were quite adaptable,* I thought, with a smile. Some species called humans Poison Worms. I laughed, and both Ul-Ro and Pheyal watched me with confusion. *Worms*, I thought with a chuckle.

Again, I would debate the worm issue another time.

"I will tell her," Pheyal said. He must have been desperate to get more time with Evie if he was willing to risk whatever reaction she might have.

"Tell me what?" Evie found us conspiring without her. Medic Ul-Ro turned his back to focus on the tablet screen of his work, and mumbling like he was busy.

I lifted a brow at Pheyal as if to say, now was the time, since we were all together now. Even Vaquel followed behind Evie. He couldn't seem to leave her alone, even after the mating heat subsided. He even worked with Medic Ul-Ro to create more toys to change her mating harness to his liking.

Vaquel whispered in her ear, "If you're good, I'll press the button." She closed her eyes, and I could hear the soft whimper as she breathed out slowly. I think knowing our mate was full of our offspring has done nothing to quench his desires. In fact, I think it's made him more needy for her.

Pheyal cleared his throat and adjusted his pants. Vaquel was an instigator, and I knew that he waited until we could hear them before teasing our little mate.

"Medic Ul-Ro has reviewed the scans of the chip BOD put in your spine, and found some news that you should know," Pheyal said with a gruff and forced statement without actually telling her anything. I sighed, and even Evie knew to look at me to finish that setup.

"Your womb has three unGor sacks attached to your walls, one of which appears to be in the process of splitting to become a fourth."

"UnGor sacks..." she repeated, not fully grasping the news. She has confessed to Vaquel many times about her fear of not being capable of growing our family. But she is mated to three unGors, and that was never a concern for us. UnGors have never had trouble creating offspring once we're bonded, but we have been suffering a disparity of females to males. All of us are hoping at least one of our offspring is female.

"Our seed is filling you with our family," Vaquel said with a lustful lick of his lips. He had every intention of making sure she dripped with more of his seed later. He's told me enough times that he thinks our seed should be in her during the whole pregnancy to help support our offspring's growth. He doesn't want a single day of her not absorbing our seed. Sometimes, I believe he forgets how long an unGor offspring takes to grow. It will be Earth years before she even shows the same bulge in her belly that Violet has after a few dan stars.

"Really?" she asked hopefully.

I nodded and smiled at her. "It is typical for an unGor to grow for five Earth years, but yes, you have four of our offspring in you."

"Two of them are mine," Vaquel claimed the twins for himself.

"All of them are ours," I corrected. Then the tough part to tell her, "Five years is a long time, and it is normal that not every offspring will make it to term."

Evie hugged her stomach protectively and her beautiful black ormete glowed. She was already bonding with them without knowing it. "All of them will make it," she demanded. I could see the way her lip trembled, and the anger mounted in her silver eyes. She had lost every offspring she's tried to carry.

"Yes, and Vaquel is a very good tactician to take care of you," I assured her. "All of us will stay with you just in case we have an egg to assist with keeping them all healthy."

Pheyal cleared his throat. "I have one."

She smiled and rushed up to him to jump into his arms. He easily caught her and lifted his ormete braid to show the swollen one underneath. Now, I understood why he was invested in making sure we told our mate about it sooner rather than later.

"Do I just eat it?" she asked, having not seen how it was given to Violet. I'd leave that explanation to Pheyal this time.

The unGor egg wiggled inside his ormete. "In a way," he began awkwardly. Then I laughed as she spasmed in Pheyal's arms, clinging to his neck as her hips rubbed his stomach. It wasn't difficult to deduce that Vaquel had pressed the button on whatever adjustments he made to the mating harness inside our mate.

Medic Ul-Ro was panting and, in his culture, it was normal to watch others during their mating rituals, but this was a private event for us, so I told Pheyal, "Let's carry our mate to our cave so you can properly give her the egg."

He grunted his agreement, and I was excited to see her reaction when he removed her harness to stuff his ormete deep inside her to gift her the egg for our offspring. One day, I'd have to tell her that I would be required to return to AsunGor. I knew that even if she chose to stay on Necias Prime with her human mates and with Vaquel and Pheyal, she would be safe—our bond was strong and supported; it could be felt across the galaxy.

I told her I'd give her everything—but in truth, it was she who gave me everything.

Thank you for reading Her Alien Delegate and supporting indie authors like me!

Please share your thoughts on this story in all the places books are shared, and join me again on another adventure. Perhaps you haven't read Riley's story in Her Alien Savior? Or you want to learn more about Roe-el and Violet's story in my free newsletter exclusive Her Alien Exchange? There are more stories in the universe with Jewel of the Alien Bandit and Her Alien Prince! Help support more books by sharing this book and others with your book buddy you think would enjoy it!

Author Note

Don't forget to help an indie author out and leave a review for other readers to find my books!

I had a lot of fun writing this book, and it helped me get over some depression and a major writing slump. What was supposed to be a shorter escape romance ended up being a full-length novel because there was more to tell for Evie, Broma and their mates Pheyal, and Vaquel. Honestly, I could have made their story three novels worth going into more of the day-to-day buildup of their relationships, and the little reveals they give each other about their past and how they all heal each other, even including POV's from each mate, but I've found that sometimes it's nice to leave some space on the page for reader's own imaginations to fill in the blanks. At least, I enjoyed the balance in this story between the story, world building, and smutty yum. Maybe, one day, if enough readers request it, I'll return to Evie, Broma, Pheyal, and Vaquel to give another story of them on AsunGor, including more POV's from the other mates. Though this story focuses on a primary mate, this delegation is very much building into a relationship of equal partnership between all mates and they will each have their place and time to shine in the group.

In the meantime, you can check out the rest of the universe with Jewel of the Alien Bandit, Her Alien Prince, Her Alien Insurgent, Her Alien Savior, Her Alien Warrior, and Her Alien Starbreaker! Check out my newly revamped website www.ste viemarie.com

It would mean a lot to me to share my stories with fellow readers and help spread the good alien peen word so that I can continue to write more stories and invest in hiring human artist to create fun character art!

You can share your thoughts on Amazon here for Her Alien Delegate: https://www.amazon.com/dp/B0FGVVL4CW

To follow along on what's coming, see teasers, progress, what I'm reading, exclusive goodies, or just say, "hi", join my newsletter and grab Her Alien Exchange e-book for freesies, or join the Sky's Smut Between the Pages on Facebook! I hang out on

Instagram more often than Twitter these days, so give me a follow: @authorsteviemarie

Thank you so much for being a fan of my alien romances, it means the world to my squishy heart.

Sky

Sky Robert is a mom of two tiny humans in training, narrates audiobooks for fantasy/sci-fi indie authors, and when she isn't writing (which is MOST of the time) you can find her consuming copious amounts of coffee, promoting indie authors, reading alien smut, fantasy, sci-fi and romance books, chowing down on Indian butter chicken, and when she actually hangs out with people in person, in real life, outside of the internet, (gasps) she's playing board or card games. All around nerd, lover of the strange, and all things fantastical. Grab your first free alien monster fated mates romance Her Alien Exchange for free when you join the Romance Newsletter:
https://sendfox.com/lp/m2gyw5

Books By Sky:
Treasures of Trillume:
Jewel of the Alien Bandit https://books.steviemarie.com/jotab
Her Alien Prince: https://books.steviemarie.com/heralienprince
Her Alien Insurgent: https://books.steviemarie.com/heralieninsurgent
Her Alien Savior https://books.steviemarie.com/heraliensavior
Her Alien Warrior: https://books.steviemarie.com/heralienwarrior
Her Alien Exchange (FREE EBOOK)
https://book.steviemarie.com/heralienexchange
Books by S.M. McCoy:
Taking Medusa: Romantasy Greek Myth Retelling
https://books.steviemarie.com/takingmedusa

See all books by Sky Robert and S.M. McCoy on:
www.steviemarie.com

Want More?

For more information about upcoming books in the Treasures of Trillume or Necia Warrior Series (or any other books by Sky Robert) like me on Facebook or subscribe to my newsletter.

Check out more books by Sky Robert at the author website www.steviemarie.com

Thanks for reading! You are a book hero!

All the squishies,

Sky

xoxo

www.ingramcontent.com/pod-product-compliance
Lightning Source LLC
La Vergne TN
LVHW020702110826
845149LV00012B/2075

* 9 7 8 1 9 6 3 6 6 9 0 2 2 *